From
# God to Goth:
# A Nine Pills Sequel

Jonny Halfhead

Copyright © 2021 Jonny Halfhead

All rights reserved.

ISBN: 9798450682716

FOR ANDY

# ACKNOWLEDGMENTS

Thanks to Martin Riley at Jexit2020, Jenny Williams at Setters Proof Reading and Editing Services, Anita, Daniel Moult, Terri, George, Susan, Mick Mercer, Elaine, Kamron, Niall, Mark O'Donnell, Goatlike Personality and most of all to my wife Helen.

# 1

## SPRING 1991, 20 YEARS OLD

How could I have possibly felt more stupid? I had never planned to be going to this cold, damp, smelly carcass of a caravan ever again. My plan had been beautiful and flawless. I had meticulously decided that my final hours would be sorrowful, yet dark, enriched and beautiful; that they would be in the squalid environment that was my static caravan home, a pitiful empty shell, furnished with one sofa chair and a very old dining table and a single wooden chair. I had filled the air with incense, Pink Floyd and the promise of eternal rest. There was to be no more pain, no more rejection, no more loneliness or isolation. I was meant to cry my final few tears and slowly and ritually consume the paracetamol laid out in neat lines before me.

If two tablets were a dose, then four would be double the dose, a dangerous amount. Over the space of time of playing a couple of vinyl albums the dosage period had stretched itself to a couple of hours. I had taken eight tablets and was easily over the limit and well on my way to a lasting and restful sleep. When I finally took the nineth pill, I was sure that I was way beyond the safe limit and onto my desired destination. Then I panicked!

As I climbed back into the caravan a few days later, I found everything as I had left it. The album on the turntable, The Cure's Disintegration on picture vinyl disc, still sat there playing a haunting echo of its ghostly shadow from a few nights before.

Seeing the remnants of one's own suicide attempt throws a harrowing reality to the eye, not just because of the shame I felt, but also the absolute embarrassment. I wanted to laugh. My stupidity and naivety were shockingly hilarious and yet at the same time tragic.

Why had I thought that nine pills were more than enough? In the cold light of day, it seemed pathetically short. Maybe if I had been four years old it would have been enough, but I was twenty. I was so sure of the amount at the time. I was facing the breath of death itself, I could feel it in my bones and on my skin. It was beautiful and at the same time extremely scary.

I felt an emotional mixture of shame and relief. Shame that I gave up, got scared and didn't follow through with what I had set out to do and at the same time, I felt relieved. It was a new moment in my life. I had stared death directly in the face and walked away unscathed. My naivety had saved me from even having to go to hospital and have my stomach pumped. I was so glad that I had asked Ivan, my rescuer and life saver, never to mention any of this to any of my family or anyone in my former congregation.

Everything in my life from that moment on, would be balanced against the face of death whose breath I had now felt. I had a chance to try and not see life as one disaster leading to another, but each obstacle and trial to overcome. I had a reference that I could use. I could do anything I could set my mind too, because next to the challenge of facing death, most challenges would be pitiful.

I was still surrounded by darkness and loneliness, but I could see another world of possibility. I just needed to try and adjust my mindset. Already my newfound freedom allowed me daring in a way I never knew possible from my former weak and fragile personality. Left in the caravan and living alone, for the first time in my life I could feel a sense of freedom and abandonment like never before. I was Jonny. I was walking a life not lived before. I was unique in the small world I knew. I was a young man that had never stood up for himself or stood up to anyone hardly at all. I had spent a life of being wrong, being a sinner, being bad and useless. That person died from an overdose of nine pills. Now I had the chance to break every single moral rule I had been brought up to blindly obey.

I had a small amount of money in my pocket, I needed bread and milk and I could get those from the local newsagent. The newsagent also likely sold pornographic magazines. For the first time in my life, I realised that I could go and buy a porn magazine from a shop. I was an adult. I had a chance to study a woman's body without remorse, shame, embarrassment or direct guilt. All I needed to do was be bold, be strong and grow up (in my own way).

The realisation of what I could do was immensely exciting. I had the power to do it. I put some change in my pocket and left the caravan with a slight skip in my step. I walked firmly and purposefully with long strides down the road. I was a tax paying grown adult with the ability to make up my own mind about the world and my place in it. It wasn't as though I hadn't seen pornographic material before.

My mind casts back to the first time I saw a pornographic magazine. It seemed that every time I think back over moments in my life, I initially remember them as harrowing and frightening experiences and yet now I could see a new perspective, bordering on hilarity.

-x-

I was in my last year at school, 16 years old. I still had no idea what a naked woman looked like. I had ideas, based on seeing a pair of boobies on the TV before my mum would hurriedly switch the channel over. Or other examples of my adult education, my mother's knitting guides or the underwear section of the shopping catalogue. Knitting guides always had models that never wore underwear no matter how lacy or loose the pattern. The only other clues where from renaissance paintings, which for some reason was art instead of pornography and ok to stare at for hours on end.

My first experience of seeing the contents of a porn mag, came from the paper round I did every morning. Each day, I would be the first to wake up and set off out of the house. I would be at the newsagents by 6am just as they were opening. I had to get there at that time as I had two paper rounds which I had to get finished before going back home and changing for school. It was always a tight schedule every day.

Being so early meant that, apart from the gorgeous girl that worked behind the till, I was the only one there. I would count and gather the papers I needed for my round underneath the rows of magazines stacked on the shelves. The top row of those magazines, barely reachable from my five-foot eight-inch height, were the adult magazines. The whole ten-foot-long shelf was rammed with stacked nudy mags that hinted at bare flesh and naughtiness. I was sixteen. Every day that I walked into that newsagents, I could feel those magazines staring down at me. I was embarrassed that they were there. Magazines made purely for men to look at and masturbate to. I wondered how any man could just walk in, pick one off the top shelf, go to the counter with the wonderfully beautiful girl serving from behind it, show her the magazine, pay and walk out with it. I had never seen anyone actually buy one, but people must, otherwise there wouldn't be so many of them on the shelves. You can't even see them very well. I know, I had tried to glance up. Each morning the pull and temptation of them would speak to me with promise of excitement and enlightenment. But I could barely bring myself to look up towards them. It befuddled me how a man could flick through each of them, weigh up which one was for him and make a choice from all the ones stacked overlapping each other all the way across the shelf. I certainly didn't want to be caught by the girl behind the counter looking up longingly at the top shelf like the sad loser I really was.

-x-

I always found it very strange how the outside world seemed so open and accepting of sex and masturbation. My mother is a strict Jehovah's Witness. They are the ones that don't celebrate Christmas, Easter, or birthdays and refuse to have blood transfusions. They also knock on people's front doors trying to convert them. I was brought up by my mother strictly in the religion, with all the rules and restrictions that came with it. I was raised with the attitude that masturbation was not just evil but leads to all sorts of strange diseases and illnesses. Pornographic magazines were created by the devil himself to lure poor teenagers into a life of debauchery and sin away from God. My head and conscience were full of God, righteousness and the doing only of good and not thinking about oneself. But I was a teenager, a teenager that adored girls but had no idea about them at all, except for the fact that they nearly all turned their noses up at me. Most girls looked at me like I was filth, or even worse, that I didn't exist at all.

-x-

Every weekday morning I would turn up at the newsagents, dutifully fight with myself to ignore that top shelf while keeping my head down and stuffing my huge newspaper bag with heavy newspapers that I would spend the next two hours carrying around the village and pushing through letterboxes. Then one day, I lost the fight with myself and decided I was going to steal one of those magazines and have a good look through it. Just thinking about it shocked me, that I was even capable of such a thought. I didn't steal anything. Stealing and lying was as bad as masturbation and fornication. I hadn't stolen a thing in my life and surely such an action at some point would end up forcing me to lie about it. I was such an evil person to even have been thinking about it.

But from the moment the thought entered my head, I couldn't get rid of it. Every day at school I would fight with myself about how trying to look at one would never work; how wrong it was and how it just wasn't worth it. The more I thought about the contents of one of those magazines, the more the plan formed in my mind, the more I was determined to take the risk. There would be two difficult stages, taking the magazine from the shelf and then having somewhere at home to store it and look at it. If there was nowhere safe to look at it, then it was pointless pinching it at all.

So, I formulated a plan.

I felt trapped. The sin was already committed even though I had not acted upon it. That just made the situation worse as now there was nothing to lose. It felt inevitable that I was going to do it and yet everything I was about to do was so wrong.

Every day since I had decided to go ahead with my evil plan, something happened to thwart the execution. Out of nowhere, another kid decided to start their round early and be at the newsagents at 6am. Then a huge intake of magazine stock came in which made the packing of the top shelf very tight. I knew with my bumbling nervous fingers that if I tried to grab one of the magazines, I would bring half the shelf down on top of me and then have to try and find a way of explaining myself! Then when days went a little smoother, the girl behind the counter wouldn't stop talking to me. That was great, female interaction was such a rarity, but she was pretty and worldly, two things that meant that I knew with certainty that she had no interest in me at all, no matter how kindly she talked to me about daily things. Then finally after days of losing gallons of nervous sweat every morning, an ideal opportunity arrived where everything seemed to just work in my favour.

I was on my own except for the lovely girl who was busy at the other end of the shop working behind the counter. It was quiet and just four feet above my head, while crouching on the floor stuffing newspapers into my huge carry bag, was the prize I was desperate to get to.

I closed my eyes, sweat pouring off my face, and built up the nerve to go for it. I jumped up onto my feet looked around to make sure the coast was clear looking like a Meercat, then stretched up on my tip toes to reach as far as I could to the top shelf. There were so many magazines to choose from. Which one do I go for? For some reason there were lots of copies of the same magazine called Fiesta. It must have been very popular and in a flash that made some sense to me. If there are lots of them it must be good. So I grabbed a copy very quickly, nearly bringing the surrounding magazines out with it, and squatted back down to the floor and stuffed the magazine into my carry bag with the rest of the newspapers.

Now I was really in it deep. I had just stolen from a shop. This was now criminal as well as immoral. My family would disown me if they found out. My congregation would ex-communicate me. I could barely say goodbye to the girl behind the counter as I left the newsagents. The two bags around my neck felt even more heavy than at any time before. I nearly collapsed when I walked outside onto the pavement and across the road to start my paper round. Every step along the road, I could feel the presence of the magazine next to my body as though it was a sheath of pure evil burning through the bag and through my clothes onto my flesh.

It wasn't until an hour into my round as one of the bags emptied that I started to get a mixture of feelings. The weight of the stolen property in my bag and on my conscience started to ease a little. I had made sure of covering every scenario that I could. I was at the furthest distance away from the shop. I had made sure to put the magazine in the second bag so that it wouldn't flop around in the empty one for an hour. I had planned that beforehand. There was no way I could have transferred the magazine from one bag to another in the street if I needed to. I had planned to cover every situation. If it was in the empty bag, there was a chance it may bounce out onto the street, or if I dropped the empty bag the magazine could fly out without anything to stop it. Sure, I was on empty streets at seven in the morning, but I knew my congregation. Anyone could be out and about and I knew all of them in the congregation and they all knew me. I couldn't risk being caught by anyone, because everyone would tell my mum anything, without exception.

I started to get more excited about the contents of the magazine the more I thought about it. What was

I going to see? I was becoming impatient to have a look, but I knew there was nowhere safe to take out a porn mag and have a look through its contents, not in this village, not with a thousand eyes everywhere. There was worse to come. I had to return to the shop first without suspicion and then get home safely where the biggest obstacle lay, somehow storing it safely at home.

When the paper round was finished, I made my way back to the shop. This was like returning to the scene of a crime. Once again, I started getting nervous and sweaty. I must have looked guilty as sin as I approached the newsagents. The magazine was now in one of my empty bags. I could feel it moving around as I walked. I feared someone in the shop would stop me and ask to look in my bag, or I feared I would trip over in a state of nervous clumsiness and the magazine would spill out. If I was exposed, my life was over. It was all too much. No matter how curious I was, it felt like the risk wasn't worth the reward anymore. If exposed, my life would change, I would be disgraced for years, if not the rest of my life.

On entering the shop, the girl behind the counter said hello and tried to strike up a friendly conversation with me and instead of acting cool, I felt the weight of embarrassment rolling about in the bottom of my delivery bag and I barely said two words and scuppered out the shop and on my way home. I must have looked very suspicious.

I slowed down on the walk home. I had nearly accomplished the impossible, but the most difficult part was yet to come. I somehow had to flawlessly get that magazine somewhere safe at home, without a hint or a chance of someone accidently or purposefully getting a hold of it. If the magazine was found at home, no-one else would be guilty except me. My mother and my sister, if they lived for a million years, would never be remotely interested in a porn mag, ever. My younger brother wouldn't have the means to get hold of something like that and at nine years old and a mummy's boy, it wouldn't even be on his radar.

My plan would have to be totally flawless, not just to smuggle in the magazine, but also to have it stored in a place where at some point, I could access it. Safe access as well. I had gone over every scenario as best I could. Anywhere in the house would be dangerous. My mother had no respect at all for my privacy, there was nothing I owned or any space that I had that was mine. Anything and everything were up for perusal and for inspection. Alongside that, my younger sister, had a full-time hobby of trying to get me into as much disfavour with my mum as she could possibly muster. It's always been the same and after 14 years of it, it's tiresome, sad and quite disturbing. Although the perfect little princess in public, for some reason my sister sees me as the target of lies, accusation, deceit and hostility without border and it's always been like that. In the outside world, she would undoubtably be a politician. She would be able to find anything I could bring into the house; she would be able to smell out guilt.

My best option for hiding the magazine was the outside storage room. This was one of two small outer rooms that were actually part of the house. One was used for coal storage to fuel the boiler. The other was used as a bike shed, tool storage and a general breeding ground for spiders. That is where I stored my filthy newspaper delivery bags, covered in newspaper print and the perfect place to store a stolen pornographic magazine. The only person likely to find anything in there was my grandfather, and he won't be looking for it.

As I approached home, the nerves once again started to shake me and I started to sweat again. There was no turning back. I figured out an hour before that none of this was worth the risk. I couldn't believe I had done this at all. It was a double sin. Theft and pornography wrapped into one, a super sin, one that would likely lead to yet another if I ever get the chance to look at its contents. That was half of the problem. I had taken all that risk and I hadn't even taken a moment to sneak a quick look by that point. I didn't dare, it would have to wait until the safest opportunity arose.

As my house came into view, I hoped beyond all hope that my mum wouldn't be at the kitchen window, or that someone from the house wouldn't appear out the front door as I approached. I knew the guilty look on my face would give me away immediately. I tried to have the plan formulated in my head and practiced it through in my mind so everything would run smoothly. I got to the house and unlocked the door to the lockup. I quickly squeezed in and stuffed the bag with the magazine down behind the bikes and then left the other bag on top of the bikes. No-one used the bikes except me, so if anyone checked the game was up already. Leaving the other bag on top of the bikes just purposefully made it more awkward to get to the offending bag. I had done all I could to cover my tracks.

I sneaked into the lockup and hesitated for a moment. The door was closed behind me to the outside world and I wondered if maybe that moment was an opportunity to grab a quick sneaky look. I poised, set between curiosity and sin, stuck in the headlights of pornographic bliss. But the risk was too high. It was early in the morning, and everyone would be in the house. It would take just one person to be curious and look in the lockup and I would be stood there caught with embarrassing trouser evidence of a sin being committed. Not the best thing to be caught in the act of teenage curiosity. So I exited the lockup, turned the key behind me and left the sinful evidence in the dark.

I felt so relieved as I entered the house. As long as I could calm my nerves down and not give the game away with my nervous demeanour, I thought I might just about get away with it.

Over the next few days, I suffered an agonising mix of torment and excitement. For the first time in my life, I had the opportunity to see a real woman's body in all its beauty and perfection. I couldn't stop thinking about it. There was an A4 sized object burning like an irradiated fireball in the bike shed and I alone knew it was there, calling to me every minute of every day. I couldn't concentrate on anything else. And yet, at the same time, it was also a loud banging drum of sin, shouting and making the most awful racket and shaking the whole house. I just felt as though it was an inevitability that someone would find it, hear that calling, the loud rumbling of sin breaking out from the outhouse.

Each day was torture. There was always somebody in the house or someone was only away for ten minutes. There just wasn't a safe moment to go and even take a quick look. Eventually the time came when no-one was around and I had the opportunity to safely take a look. I locked myself in the bike shed. Even though it seemed safe that no-one would come back home, there was still a chance that my grandad could be passing by and let himself in. I had an excuse prepared, I was tidying up the shed and didn't want to be hit by the door that opened inwards. That was a great excuse for having the door locked with me inside. I couldn't chance taking the magazine inside the house, that would be suicide.

I was close to losing consciousness. The split of terror and fear along with pure teenage arousal and adrenaline was making me so anxious, I couldn't help but feel sick.

The thrill and excitement was all encompassing as I opened the magazine in such a greedy way that I turned straight to the middle pages. I almost fell over from shock onto the dirty concrete floor in a loud crash as I steadied myself against the bicycles filling up the room. I couldn't believe it, women have hair on their vaginas!

I was so shocked and couldn't work out if I felt appalled or aroused. The women's skin, curves, breast and bodies were so beautiful and amazing, but I still couldn't work out at the age of sixteen, why I didn't know that women have pubic hair. Children and renaissance paintings don't have pubic hair.

After half an hour of intense study and the sin of self-relief, the reality of my sin hit home and I felt the urgency to get rid of the evidence. If it took days to look at it, I feared it would likely take weeks to have a chance to safely dispose of the magazine. I went back into the house, once my trousers allowed me to walk straight, and hurriedly grabbed the dustbin bag from the kitchen. I took the bag into the bike shed and stuffed the magazine down to the bottom of the trash bag after one last look through first. Then in a flash I emptied the main dustbin outside and stuffed the kitchen rubbish down at the bottom and filled everything else on top of it.

It was all over. I decided - never again!

## -X-

That was then. That was the even more naive Jonny. That was the old life. Now I was an adult. Now I was no longer constrained by the rules of my former religion. Now I could shape my own life and my own destiny. And on this new journey, I decided I was going to use my adult freedom to legitimately purchase a porn mag.

I walked into the shop, picked up bread and milk and casually perused the magazine shelf. There were still so many magazines to choose from and I could not see what they were. My newfound confidence only reached so far. I didn't fancy going through all the magazines one after the other looking for the right choice. So, I just confidently reached out and grabbed any random magazine. I took my collection to the till and it was only then that I realised that it was a lady working at the till.

I fought with myself internally. She must see loads of men buying pornographic magazines. Judging by the number of mags on the shelf, they must be as popular as cigarettes. With head held high I put the goods on the counter and felt the warm glow of my nervous but confident face and paid the lady and left.

I was so grown up….

## 2

## LATE SUMMER 1989, 18 YEARS OLD

I was a pariah. Damaged goods.

I was eighteen, still living at home with my mum, sister and brother. I was still going to the church meetings three times a week. Still knocking on people's doors at the weekends, trying to convince them to convert to a religion that I had so many doubts about myself. It didn't seem like a choice that I had to go and do these things. My mum had made it very clear that if I didn't go to all the meetings and I didn't go knocking on doors at least for ten hours a month, I would have to leave the house and live somewhere else. I didn't know anything else. I had been brought up in this religious cocoon. I was supposedly part of a larger family and yet I was bordering on the outskirts of it. I was on the fringes.

This was a constant threat from my entire

extended family. If I was not in, then I was out. If I was out, then I was all the way out. Out of the congregation, out of blessing with God, out of my family home, out on the street. The view I had of the outside world had been coloured completely by the Jehovah's Witnesses organisation that I belonged to. All I saw of the real outside world were the people in my workplace.

I worked in a warehouse for a company that quarried natural stone. One of the managers was a Jehovah's Witnesses and got me the job. That immediately put many people's backs up in the company, because I was favoured in some small way. I didn't feel favoured at all. Working in the stores was the worst place to be. The production people hated you because you're seen as part of the management, the management look down on you because you work in overalls in the muck and dust and not in a suit in the office. Those were the days of YTS, the glorious Youth Training Scheme. The cheapest form of labour. I was earning £28.50 a week for a full-time job, working alongside people that earn ten times more. The Youth Training Scheme replaced apprenticeships and they were no replacement at all and just became a method of deploying modern slavery. Once a fortnight, I was sent to a training facility in the town to work towards a qualification, the level of the qualification would be practically worthless to any employee afterwards.

In addition to working in no man's land as a stores person, I was one of Jehovah's Witnesses. I didn't swear, I didn't get involved in the sexist wolf whistles pointed at the female office staff, I didn't do the Christmas, Easter or birthday celebrations. I didn't lie, cheat or steal. That put a target on me as a centre of ridicule and practical jokes. I also never involved myself with anyone outside of work either, that association was forbidden by my religion. Each day that I went to work, I was a pariah, an outcast, a point of hatred, ridicule and suspicion. I hated going to work!

When I went home, the situation was not much better.

Two years previously, I had the most beautiful and loving experience with a girl when I stayed at her parents' house for a week. But because it was a sexual experience, even though it didn't involve sex and even though I wasn't baptised in the religion (and I'm still not baptised even now), I got heavily punished for it. I spent months, shamed and humiliated in front of the whole congregation. I was stripped of all responsibilities. I was treated as though I was disfellowshipped. For months, as a punishment for my wrongdoing, no-one was allowed to talk to me. All my friends had to pretend I didn't exist. My family had nothing to do with me. Even the family in the house limited their association with me. Three times a week, I would still have to go to church and sit at the back, not being allowed to say anything to anyone. Finally, after months of humiliation, I was accepted back into the congregation. Only I wasn't accepted. I was marked. I was damaged goods, a man with a chequered past, someone to be wary of and watched carefully for any signs of badness and recurrence of immorality.

It took a long time to get accepted back into the congregation. It felt as though I didn't have a choice. I had no life at all outside the congregation. I knew no-one, not even the folk I used to go to school with. Everyone outside was bad association and had to be avoided at all costs.

Even now, my mother doesn't approve of my current existence. I am an embarrassment, a shameful rebellious teenager that brought the ultimate shame to the family. I'm certainly not a man that had shared the most beautiful and loving experience of my life with someone I wanted to devote myself to, instead I am dirty and selfish.

I looked around the congregation and saw many men that lived their lives solitary and alone. Some of them were once leaders and because of mistakes and errors that were supposed to have been forgiven, they acted as reminders of former glories and consequences of wrongdoing. All I could see for myself was a life reflected in their sorrow and isolation. My mother watched my every move with suspicion and disgust. She thought of me as a pervert. I had neither the confidence nor the freedom to even look at a woman and I presumed I never would.

There was a good lesson learned at school. It was impossible to be cool or to fit in when being a fully developed and devoted Jehovah's Witness. Bullying, name-calling and beatings were a daily occurrence. If you did fit in, that was a bad sign that you were part of the outside world. Standing out as being different was a testament to being a true believer. It took many years of school and extreme bullying and a desperation to just fit in, in any way that I could. I eventually decided to embrace my differences and instead of being ashamed, actually build upon them. It was good to be different. In fact, because other kids around me didn't understand the path I was moving to, the bullying started to relax a little, only a little, but enough to allow me to breathe.

I was starting to get to that same space again. I had a deep creative streak that I tapped into, which gave me another level to work with and explore. The combination of being reclusive, secluded, marginalised and held on the fringes of every walk of life along with a new found creativity gave me fuel for rebellion. I wasn't out and out rebellious of course, I was scared to do anything truly rebellious, I just used little things to expand myself and try and become more unique, more myself, prouder, if any pride is even possible under such oppression.

-x-

Uniformity is the key in the Jehovah's Witness society. There are Bible rules, Witness society rules, local culture rules, congregation rules and family rules. Layer upon layer of expectancy, moral conduct and formula to follow and abide by - all of which have variable punishments. There isn't a law in the Bible that says you cannot smoke, but the Jehovah's Witnesses society as a whole does not allow smoking which is punishable by disfellowshipping. In the congregation I belonged to, music that has drumming is very much frowned upon. Drums are the instrument of the devil, put into music to make youngsters gyrate and move their hips provocatively, which leads to sexual attraction and fornication. I found many of these rules hilarious, comical even. I'd be tempted to laugh out loud at hearing a mention of such ideas, except that would just make for even more trouble for disrespecting those in the congregation who are wiser and more knowledgeable of the temptations of the world. Weddings in the congregation didn't have discos for that reason, instead we had barn dances and classical music playing, or the Jehovah's Witness hymns.

In such an oppressive environment, any rebellion was going to have to be done in little steps. My friends could rebel more than I could. They had more liberal parents that didn't take some of the smaller moral issues such as drums in music as seriously. I had a strict mother. My uncle would warn her about being too strict with me. "If you tighten a spring down too tightly, it will go so much further when it is set free," he would say. But my mum wouldn't have any of it. I had been given a small amount of freedom a couple of years before and I had abused it. I was the lesson for never trusting your child with anything or anywhere ever again. I was almost a write off, beyond help and beyond any redemption just because I had committed one sin and then paid for it in full.

-x-

I started to love music. Music that belonged to me personally and not what was fed to me like milk from a teat. I became hungry for music that spoke to me at my level, that understood my pains and suffering. I had lost the biggest love of my life. I had no idea where she was, who she was with. I had been in emotional agony after having such an intense and loving experience and I didn't even know if she was alive anymore. I know so little about her life now. I wasn't allowed any contact and as much as I wanted to rebel against that rule, it was one rule I feared the most to break and wanted to break. I sought out music that reflected my isolation, my heartbreak, my deep, deep despair, alienation and rejection.

My musical journey started with the few people I knew that had records that you could class as outside of the norm. My uncle had records from the early seventies that weren't exactly easily accessible pop. I had listened to a lot of pop music, although the radio was on at work all the time and everyone I knew listened to pop music, it just didn't connect with me other than in a fleeting, passive way. My uncle's old records did connect with me for some reason. He had an album by Budgie, a couple of Emerson, Lake and Palmer records and also Jean Michel Jarre's first album Oxygene. At first, they seemed just weird, almost noise that I could barely hear any tune from, but then I started to hear much more than I heard in pop music.

As soon as I started to listen to those records, my mum had problems with them. I used the fact that they were my uncle's records as a defence for the legitimacy of listening to them. For a while that worked and kept my mum off my back about my music. My mum didn't have a clue about music at all. Her records consisted of Hooked on Classics, snippets of classical tunes backed by a drab disco beat. She had a Cliff Richard love songs album, a best of The Monkees album and a couple of ABBA records. The ABBA records got thrown out though because she thought they were bringing a demonic influence into the house at one point. My mum once bought a double album of cover songs. It was comprised of about 300 pop songs, all played mashed together one after the other in ten second bursts. It was an awful album, but my mum was so happy. "Look 300 songs for that price, it's a bargain!"

When I bought my first album by Ultravox, it transformed the house in my opinion. I was so hungry for new music. I would go around the houses of the people in the congregation and try and look through their record collections. The more colourful people in the congregation always had superior record collections. I started to buy second-hand albums from record fairs. It meant I could afford to experiment and try new things out. The more unusual the music from my bedroom, the more annoyed my mother got. My music had drums in it and heavy guitars, both instruments of the devil. Knowing my mother thought that ABBA brought in demons into the house, I knew I couldn't rely on her twisted ideas of what music was morally. Whenever my mother would confront me about my music as my tastes expanded, the more I asked her to trust my instincts as she didn't have a clue about the subject at all. I tried to explain that God doesn't think that crows are a lesser animal because they don't sing out beautiful whistles all the time. All God's creations are beautiful in their own way. How can a sound be good or bad? That was a concept I just couldn't understand at all.

I was also finding a new love of classical music. Another artist from the seventies that was just as innovative in electronic music as Jean Michel Jarre was Isao Tomita. He performed classical music in a very colourful and beautiful way using synthesizers. I was appreciating the music of Kraftwerk as well, but Kraftwerk and Wendy Carlos were the equivalent of 'Black and White' pictures next to the 'Full Colour' of Isao Tomita. None of that music sat well with the people around me though. To many it really did sound like the devil's own music.

I couldn't afford to keep buying records though, even second-hand ones. I certainly couldn't risk buying an album I had never listened to before with the hope that I would like the music. My saving grace was the town's library. Suddenly out of nowhere, the main library in the centre of town started to lend out records as well as books. I could borrow an album, record it onto cassette and if it was not to my taste I could record over the cassette with another album. If I liked the album enough, I would go and buy it. Most of the music I had been listening to was from the seventies as there was little exposure to new music that I could find. Top of the Pops was always on a Thursday night when I was in Church. Any other music programmes on TV were either on too late at night or I would never have been allowed to watch them anyway on the one television we had in the living room. My only other source for hearing new music was the radio. I tried to listen to John Peel, but it was always on late and I either had work or preaching to do the next day. When I did push myself to listen to it, I would usually fall asleep.

The town library opened up so much new music that really spoke to me and connected with me at a very deep level. The Fall, The Cult, The Cure, Sisters of Mercy, The Mission, Cocteau Twins, I couldn't get enough of the amazing music that was around. Every piece of music I was hearing was a new and amazing sensation of discovery. I started to obsess with the word 'goth.' It seemed that so much of the music I was connecting to was labelled goth music, except that every band with that label, hated it immensely.

I knew that some people thought of goth music as devil music, a sort of Satan worshipping form of music. I never made the connection myself. There was a Hammer Horror type of iconography which I found very fascinating. I had been careful to make sure I didn't bring any demon influence into the house through my music. The fear of demons and bad spirits is very real to me, as real as my belief in God. Sometimes I find the limit to my boundaries and I have to question myself. I did this when I came across a band called Fields of The Nephilim. This was a band that scared me. They were deeply rooted in Paganism and Pagan symbolism. The lead singer Carl Mcoy had the deepest, weirdest, scariest vocal style I had ever heard. I also knew who the Nephilim were from the Bible stories about Noah and the flood. They were sons of fallen angels. So the band was named after a group of beings very close to demons. It was all too much for me and I took those records straight back to the library and never recorded them.

-x-

The Cult were a band that played psychedelic rock on their Love album and around this time the amazing follow up Electric came out and I couldn't stop playing it. It was an album I had to buy. It was so raw, so well produced, had an endless amount of energy and power and had a texture that was both sharp and warm. I loved it.

The album was released in a gatefold sleeve and had a poster of the band inside the sleeve. The poster had the band posing together, the singer Ian Astbury adorned in Native American clothes. He was such a pretty boy. Around the poster were the words 'The Cult' and 'Electric' in an amazing tooth shaped biting font, a design I just found incredible and captured the sound of the album so well. The whole poster was striking, but the font was the part that captured my imagination the most. It captured the texture of the music so well. I had done Technical Drawing and Art at school and that font appealed to my design aesthetic and it opened my eyes as to how music and art can sit side by side with each other if the right essence is captured.

I liked the poster so much that I stuck it on my bedroom wall alongside my paintings and drawings. I couldn't stop looking at it and the intricacies of the font style and Ian Astbury's furry hat.

It only took a few hours before my mum saw the poster on the wall. It amazed me how quickly my mum noticed changes in my bedroom. I was 18 years old and my bedroom was my own private space away from all the bullshit outside, including my prying mum's suspicious eyes and crazy opinions. That obviously was not how my mum saw it. Even though I paid ninety percent of my earnings to my mum as board, it earned me no privacy at all and I was constantly reminded that I lived in her house and had no rights to anything, especially privacy. To my mother, privacy breeds sin. "If you have nothing to hide, you have no need for privacy."

I went into my bedroom and caught my mum already in there standing in the middle of the room starring at the poster on my wall, her face turning purple with ever increasing anger and steam almost pouring from her ears like a crazy cartoon character.

I knew that, as seen by the Jehovah's Witnesses, posters of pop stars were a form of idolatry. I knew that having a poster of a band on my wall would, to the casual observer, look like I was in awe of the people in the poster. I knew the truth of why it is on my wall and I was comfortable with that reason. I didn't feel the need to explain that it was because it was a piece of art, that it was sitting on the wall next to my own artwork. I did know how it looked to my mother.

"What is that doing on your wall?" my mother spat out with an intense anger as she pointed at the poster.

I was ready to explain my reasoning, although mostly to try and get her to calm down and stop boiling and spitting rather than any need to clear myself of wrongdoing. I had given up on trying to constantly explain myself to my mum. Everything I did, my every action and my every word was full of evil intent and demonic sin as far as my mum was concerned. I was a devil boy, fuelled by any tale that my sister would care to make up, which she constantly and frequently did.

"How dare you bring demons into this house!" she shouted furiously waving her finger at the picture on the wall.

"You're not even trying to hide it anymore, rip down that filth right now!"

It only took a moment to see the spluttering rage in my mother's face and gestures and a glance at the familiar poster on the wall to realise what she was actually referring to. It wasn't the band in the picture per se, or the clothes that they were wearing, or the fact that I had an idol on my wall that was at the forefront of my mother's anger.

"Oh," I suddenly realised, trying so very hard not to laugh. "It's the word 'Cult' isn't it?"

I struggled to believe it as I said it out loud, but I knew my mother's twisted and simple-mindedness.

"You are letting the occult directly into this house!" she shouted in anger, fear and accusation.

I couldn't help myself and I started to laugh, an action which just enraged my mother even more.

"Ha ha, 'occult' is a completely different word to 'cult,'" I said calmly and slowly, trying not to laugh too much.

I felt a lot calmer knowing that it had just been a misunderstanding.

"This is why you should let me regulate my music myself and give me some trust that I know what I'm doing," I said back to my mum.

"Don't you use such a condescending tone with me," my mother shouted, still spitting with anger and frustration. "I know what a cult is and it's satanic."

"No mum," I said as calmly as I could.

I stopped laughing as I could see that once again my mother just didn't have the intelligence to understand and already I knew I was going to lose this one.

"A cult is just a following of people, a group that follow or believe in the same thing. Jehovah's Witnesses are a cult as we all follow the same thing."

I could see in my mum's eyes that she didn't believe me at all, I could also see how annoyed with herself she was that she didn't really understand what I was saying. She was quite obviously annoyed with me calling the Jehovah's Witnesses a cult as well.

"The 'Truth' has nothing to do with the occult at all. I really wonder what is happening with you, daring to call God's organisation devil worshippers!"

and with that she pulled down the poster from my bedroom wall and ripped it up in front of me.

"This needs to be burned to destroy the demons," she announced.

I had seen this before with the ABBA records. You can't throw a demon possessed object into the dustbin and risk someone else picking it up and getting the evil influence. Such an object should be destroyed totally.

It was experiences like this that made me question what kind of an organisation I belonged to. I had been having serious doubts about the organisation we all called 'the Truth.' I was split between two arguments. On the one hand I could see the facts: Jehovah's Witnesses are the only organisation to work out the code in the Bible that clearly shows that we are living in the End Times. Armageddon will be here so very soon, that is the name of God's war where he will destroy all those not associated with Jehovah. I was teetering on the border of God's approval and damnation. I feared that I may be on the side of death when judgement comes.

-x-

In the late 19th century, Jehovah's Witnesses predicted that the beginning of the 'Last Days' would start in 1914. The code in the Bible shows that there would be 2520 years between the fall of

Jerusalem and the start of the Last Days. They predicted this before 1914 and they were right. The last days would be marked with unprecedented wars, famines, pestilences and earthquakes like none in history. They quote scholars that agree that the 20th Century has been the worst in history for all these signs of the end. The Bible says that those that witnessed 1914 would not die before the end would come. It's 1989, I'm in the very last throws before the end will come. This is all fact. Absolute proven truth. That realisation filled me with fear and dread, because I also had doubts.

Only a few days before, I tried to ask the most cutting questions that were tearing my insides apart. My grandmother was the centre of all wisdom and spiritual information and so the best person to ask my fundamentally important questions. I couldn't understand where evil came from. If God created all things, then surely, he created evil and wrongdoing. Why would he do that? If choice is God-given, the greatest gift from him, then to use that gift and be punished for using that gift is surely cruelty itself? My greatest questions were about the whole concept of what I perceived the Bible to be about. If man lost paradise and eternity through sin, and Jesus paid back that sin by dying for our inherited sins, who created this whole game of rules and laws? How can the loss of eternal life be paid by the death of another? Who made that rule and why does it make sense to everyone else and not me?

I was going out every week knocking on people's

doors to preach to them. It was what was required of me to be a faithful Jehovah's Witness. I understood the urgency to try and save people's lives and save them from being killed in the impending Armageddon. But without the answers to these fundamental questions, how am I expected to have enough conviction to persuade a total stranger that what I have is the truth? These questions were holding me back and stopping me from immersing myself wholeheartedly into The Truth. But nobody could answer my questions with any answers that made sense. My grandmother would give me stock answers that I had heard a thousand times which didn't clear anything up at all and just muddied the waters, like smoke and mirrors. When pushed, my grandmother would just get angry and tell me that I needed to have faith and just believe.

"If only you would just trust in Jehovah and throw yourself into his love," she would say. But my faith in the people that did God's will made me question things even more. I saw so many lies, so much politics, so much corruption that I struggled to let that all go and just 'believe.'

No-one had any answers. I was so desperate for them that I went around asking everyone and I'd been warned about asking those type of questions. They were apostate questions. That hurt me greatly. Whenever I tried to do the right thing, it felt like I just got thrown back down again, back into a pit of despair and isolation. My faith was constantly being attacked from inside The Truth and my independence and determination to be unique built up. It was the only pride I had. An artist's pride.

A person's clothing in the congregation was seen as a reflection of a person's faith. Women must wear skirts, knee length and no higher. Women must also not wear anything too tight or revealing. Men must have short hair, that meant hair that did not reach the ears or shirt collar. A man having long hair would be too feminine and might persuade someone to become homosexual and homosexuality is a filthy and disgusting sin in the eyes of Jehovah's Witnesses. Beards were also severely frowned upon. We were meant to emulate Jesus who very likely had a beard, and yet for some strange reason, beards were banned.

The whole set of written and unwritten rules sent my mind in a spin. Every time I asked who created and decided these rules, the answers that came back to me were, 'because we represent Jehovah and his organisation, so we should look professional and respectable and at the same time, we are not to be any part of a world that is going to be ending soon, so following fashions or trends is to be part of the world.'

Like with so many things in the 'Truth', reasons and arguments were dished out like formless regurgitations. I was sure that most of the time, the people that spurted out these reasons were not thinking about what they were saying or the arguments behind them. They just didn't make any sense at all. Every time I questioned these standard retorts, I was shot down in a flurry of fear, panic and annoyance. The answers given were so weak.

To be no part of the world meant that in a crowd, you should be able to spot the Jehovah's Witness. But that just wasn't the case. In fact, standing out in a crowd as being different was actually frowned upon as well. If I looked different, I was drawing attention to myself, which was seen as a form of self-worship and diverted attention from God. I knew these arguments as I had spent a lifetime hearing them, but when it actually came to really understanding them, the rules made no sense at all, they contradicted other rules. I wanted to do the right thing, I wanted to be a good Christian, but I was finding that no matter what I did, I was always in the wrong. So I was supposed to analyse myself further, which just confused the sets of rules even more.

For instance, the length of a man's hair. I kind of understood the rules from a simplistic point of view. Jehovah's Witnesses believe that there are two simple genders, male and female. These are God given genders and the world likes to play around with them and mix them up. This leads to sin, sexual immorality and homosexuality. Therefore, two strictly distinct genders. That is why men should have short hair, so they do not look feminine. But doesn't that also mean that women should have long hair? But there wasn't a rule for that. My own mother had short hair, surely that made my mother look like a man? Then of course who decides how long a man's hair should be? Does the Bible decide? No, it doesn't, anywhere. There are no direct instructions in the Bible that define what length of hair is long and what length of hair is acceptable. So where did the rules about hair not growing over the ears or reaching the shirt collar come from? How where these two rules decided? I did ask this question and the answer was, "what is acceptable in society as smart." The same benchmark was also used for clothes. In order to not bring God's people into any reproach, they must look like they are conforming and being responsible citizens.

But that was the standard of the world, the world that we were supposed to be no part of. We used the trends and standards of the world to dictate our own rules. One argument I put forward, was that in the seventies, flared trousers and kipper ties were the excepted norm in the congregation dress sense and weren't questioned. In fact, to wear drainpipe trousers and shoelace ties would be drawing attention to oneself and the Elders would be having a word with you about your attire. And yet now, ten years or more further on, the total opposite was true. I had seen some men in the congregation reprimanded because of their 'out of date' attire, wearing big flared trousers and fat kipper ties, when the accepted norm is drainpipe trousers and thin ties. Those trends were decided and dictated by the fashion industry of the world, the world that we were to be no part of.

I got into trouble for asking that question.

My friends in the congregation tried to bend the rules without breaking them. They would grow their hair long on the top and have their hair tapered to shaven at their ears to technically be correct. I just wanted to be myself as much as I dared. So, I shaved all my hair down to a crew cut. I got told off for that too. I looked like a 'skinhead thug', I was told. I was getting sick of trying to conform to rules that made no sense.

I didn't have much money, so I began to have respect for the punk ethic of 'do it yourself.' One of the Elders used to wear a dark red suit jacket. It really matched his personality. The jacket was a little bit Teddy Boy-ish. It did look old on him, like it was his favourite in the sixties but kept on wearing it more through habit than any aesthetic. I knew I could wear it with a new attitude that would bring it back to life. I didn't need to change anything on it, just having it worn on my young shoulders would be enough to bring it back to its prime again. I confronted the Elder and told him how much I loved his dark red jacket and asked if I could buy it off him and that I would look after it and wear it with pride. To my excitement and astonishment he agreed to sell it to me and the transaction was completed.

The first time I wore it to church, my mother told me outright that I wasn't allowed to wear it, she said I was drawing to much attention to myself with it on.

I told her who I had bought it off, she had seen the Elder wearing it for years, so I defied her and told her she couldn't start telling me what to wear as well as everything else in my life. So, I wore it to church.

Two Elders had words with me about wearing that dark red suit jacket. I explained to them who I had bought it off, that they had seen that same jacket for years on one of their fellow Elders without issue, but they still insisted that I was in the wrong.

I ignored them!

Instances like that just proved to me that in order to have any personality, I was going to be a pariah even more than I already was in the congregation. So, I just tried to find my own way, going against the tide. After that incident I bought a dinner jacket with shiny lapels and a gorgeous suit from Burton's. The Burton's suit had a very feminine cut and didn't hang any lower than the trouser belt line. It was light grey and all the pockets had a bright silver zip across the top of each of them. Anyone older than me hated the suit and because of that I loved it. I found it fascinating that something as benign as a piece of material could cause so much anger and negative attitude. The material is what it is, a piece of cloth to keep myself warm and modest. Everything else is politics, manipulation, envy and control.

-x-

I was living two simultaneous lives totally entwined within each other and it was causing me so much heartache, confusion and great pain. I was fearful of God, of judgement, of Armageddon and being alone for the rest of my life. I was also becoming more daring, more rebellious, sicker of the contradictions and the opposing rules and in so finding parts of me that are colourful amongst a very dull black and white personality.

# 3

## SUMMER 1991, 20 YEARS OLD

I was very nervous for several reasons. I'd never really travelled on my own very much. Even at 20 years old, I couldn't drive, I very rarely used buses, never got the train and travelling on a coach was unheard of. I'd spent so many years on a road bike, the peddling and not the motored type, that I went everywhere on that instead of using public transport. I wish I'd been able to drive. I took driving lessons a few months previously when I lived at home with my mum, but then I lived in a completely different world. When my mother threw me out, the driving lessons had to stop so I could afford to feed myself and pay the rent. My bike went from being a pleasure to being my sole means of transport, killing my love of cycling in the process.

My new sense of purpose forced me to go way beyond my comfort zone in all aspects of my life. Since my suicide attempt a few months previously, my new perspective on my world and life now enabled me to see with new eyes. I thought I was close to death, so everything now had a comparison with death itself. There was a realisation that most things won't kill me, so what was I afraid of?

-x-

The previous year had been so much of a rollercoaster. Shortly before being thrown out of home, my independence had become far too rebellious for those around me. As I look back, it seemed like a joke. When in such a stifling and controlling environment like the Jehovah's Witnesses, any little action seemed like a massive shout out against the strain of control and manipulation. The little nuances of change in clothing habits made a big impact on the way that people in the congregation dealt with me. Many in the congregation had little to do with me, partly because of my disciplinary some years before which tarnished me as bad association. Since that experience and my doubts and questions of doctrine and observations of those around me who were supposed to be the 'good' people and their lies, deceit and double standards, I became more and more on the fringes of the congregation.

I loved my music and at home I would spend all my time locked up in my bedroom listening to all sorts of music for hours and hours. It meant that I wasn't properly studying in preparation for church three times a week, which meant I wasn't so ready to participate either. I didn't have too much time anyway in between full-time work and going to church and preaching. So, I tried to best use my time for things that really meant something deeply to me and my music fulfilled that.

-x-

I went out one day with my grandmother on the preaching work. My grandmother regularly saw a young couple that she was conducting a Bible study with, and she took me long with her. They were only a couple of years older than I was. He was holding down an office job and was smart, good looking and had very respectable short hair. He welcomed us into his house in a very well-mannered and polite way. They lived in a small terrace house which was sparsely furnished and looked quite poor and scruffy.

As we went through the house to the living room, sitting on the sofa was the man's girlfriend. She had the most beautiful of faces, so much so that I instantly gasped at the site of her. But this encounter was something completely new to me as she was adorned with a look that took my breathe away. She wore a black lacy dress with tight black Lycra leggings, loads of silver belts, bangles, necklaces, amazing thick eyeliner that spread across her face in fascinating artistic patterns and finally she had jet black hair that was very wild, backcombed and spikey. Her hair surrounded her beautiful face and framed it as wide as her shoulders in a complete circle. They call the style gothic and she was the most beautiful woman I had ever seen. I was blown away. I spent the whole Bible study trying not to stare, but at the same time not being able to stop looking at her and studying every single line, curve and the style of her face and make up.

The couple's Bible study lasted for a few months. My grandmother managed to convince them both that they were living in sin, because they slept together without being married and if they wanted to become Jehovah's Witnesses, the first thing they needed to do was to get married. So, they quietly got married at a registry office. They didn't end up joining the Jehovah's Witnesses and the Bible studies eventually stopped. Both became fans of the Rave scene and she chopped all her beautiful dark hair off. She was still one of the most beautiful women I had have ever met, but the gothic style transformed her beauty to an ethereal level that I completely fell in love with. She would never have been allowed to be a Jehovah's Witness with that style of dress, make-up and hair. No matter how much of an artist one is, decorating the palate of self is just not tolerated in the congregation.

-x-

That experience encouraged me to explore the gothic more and more. That put me on a collision course for my current situation, estranged from my family and all my friends and now living in a caravan. It was my love of the band The Cure that made me want to see them live. That love of The Cure's music led me to go to my first concert to see them even though my mum told me that at 19 years old I wasn't allowed to go. It was that final act of rebelling that caused my mother to throw me out. It was throwing me out that made me realise that I couldn't be a Jehovah's Witness anymore. It was because I stopped going to church three times a week that my family and all my friends turned their backs on me and decided they were not allowed to have anything to do with me anymore. It was the chain reaction that led me here, just from the love of a form of music and music culture.

Back then, I already loved a lot of the popular music I knew, but I found myself on a quest to find out what defined the gothic style and to try and find more music that belonged to what seemed at first a very underground music scene.

-x-

In the seventies and eighties, punk had changed the music scene in the UK. Record companies that released music to the world were usually big multinational companies that ripped off the artists financially and even artistically. In the late seventies loads of small, independent record labels started up to support punk, metal and loads of small music subcultures. It got to a point where you could rely on a record label to fit your music tastes. Quite by accident I realised that a lot of bands I liked where on the same small independent record label called 4AD. It was amazing how much good music I was already listening to was on this one record label. Bauhaus, Cocteau Twins, Pixies and Lush were all on 4AD. I had picked up a compilation album called 'Lonely is an Eyesore' around 1988 which intrigued me greatly. The style of the album was incredible. The texture and font and fold out style of the sleeve was so creative and clever. But most of all it was finding that album that made me realise how much of the music of the label I already liked. The album also had a full run down of all the releases from the label since its start in 1980. Amongst the bands listed were a couple I recognised as being gothic and I hadn't heard their music. They were Clan of Xymox and Dead Can Dance. All I could think about was how many of those other bands listed were gothic in their style and I was starting to trust the label's taste. I wanted to go and sample as much of the music listed on that album.

That started my love affair with the record label 4AD. They had been at the forefront of graphic design in the eighties and the covers of their releases were just breathtaking and so very clever and representative of the texture and style of the music within. After listing to 'Lonely is an Eyesore' on repeat for months, I managed to pick up albums by Clan Of Xymox and Dead Can Dance. Both bands were just the most amazing music that I had ever heard. It re-enforced my love of the gothic genre, and it gave me such a hunger to search for more goth bands.

Then quite by accident, I was looking through the music books at John Menzies, a large newsagent in the centre of town. Searching for books about goth bands was really difficult. They seemed to be so underground that the general music press just didn't seem to cover the genre and when they did, they ripped it to pieces. To my shock, on the shelves at John Menzies was a thick black book by a writer called Mick Mercer. It was called 'Gothic Rock, All you ever wanted to know...but were too gormless to ask.' It was an encyclopaedia of all the current and historic bands labelled as goth (whether they liked it or not). For me this was like finding a huge block of gold just lying there with a tiny price tag on it. I bought it there and then and couldn't get home quick enough to read through it.

The book was a revelation. Not only did it list all the classic goth bands with a little history of each, it also had bands listed from all around the UK that were currently active, with their contact addresses. I could actually write a letter and send it in the post to any one of those bands around the country. Goth felt so accessible. The book also listed fanzines from around the country and their contact details. Fanzines are small home-made magazines made by a fan for fans. They really were in the punk spirit of 'anyone can do it.' The whole of Mick Mercer's book was a treasure trove. It was packed with photos throughout and the most outrageously dressed from inside a book of extreme fashion was a character called Jonny Slut from a band called

Specimen. Jonny Slut had a huge black mohican standing more than a foot tall above his head, eyeliner decorating his eyes and all over the side of his shaven head, his body was adorned in ripped tights, fishnets, leather, Lycra, belts, chains and ripped up t-shirts. He was equally horrifying and immensely beautiful at the same time.

Setting aside the photographs of stunning visuals and beautiful people, the book also interviewed goth fans themselves from around the UK. The fans expressed why they loved all things gothic. Old Hammer horror films, gothic architecture, Victoriana, pre-Raphaelite art, the new romantic poets like Shelley and Byron, medieval romance and chivalry. Everything they talked about really connected with me and I found that I was already a goth deep in my soul without even knowing it. The book made me want to find these kindred spirits and share a passion with them.

Buying that book changed my life, yet again.

I formulated a life plan. I wanted to be a part of this scene and to meet these deeply romantic and artistic people. I wanted to fall in love with many, not one and share the unbound love and passion I felt so strongly inside myself. The best way to do that I thought was to be in a goth band. The book and the punk ethic demonstrated to me that I could do that, it was in my reach. When compared to the spectre of death, a spectre I had faced, it was attainable. Being in a goth band was not going to kill me.

I couldn't play an instrument though. I owned a bass guitar. I had dabbled with it for a year or so and although I could play along to a few songs by The Cure and a Bauhaus song, I struggled with a comfortable technique. I wasn't going to be able to get into a band through any musical talent. So instead, I formulated a progression plan. If I could get involved in the scene somehow, I might be able to meet like-minded people that would be interested in forming a band, and with enough artistic desire and style I could achieve anything.

As I looked through the Mick Mercer Gothic Rock book, I picked up on all those homemade fanzines and decided that was my way in. If I wrote a fanzine and interviewed bands and went out and met goths, then maybe If I was enough of a creative artist, I could find a way in.

I wrote out a plan to create a goth fanzine. I bought an old typewriter that weighed half a ton. I started to write to all the bands in the Gothic Rock book and asked them if I could do an interview with them, especially if they were touring somewhere nearby where I could meet them face to face. I had a tape cassette player that was quite large but had detachable speakers. If I took the cassette player with me without the speakers, I could use the built-in microphone to record the interviews. I had a good quality SLR camera that I had bought a year or so before which I could take photos with. The only thing I was missing was a way to print the fanzine and a place to sell them.

I got in touch with Ivan. Ivan was the man I rang when I took those nine pills. He let me recover at his house. He helped me move house more than once. Out of all the Jehovah's Witnesses that abandoned me out of a sense of 'tough love' (an attempt to get someone back to church by shunning them and leaving them abandoned to tempt them back in again), Ivan was the one that regularly dropped in on me to check if I was ok. He owned a small spring factory and in his office he had a photocopier. I offered to pay him per sheet to photocopy from a master that I would create. To my surprise he agreed to help me. I knew he would have to keep it quiet, if the Elders in the congregation learned he was going far from shunning me by actually helping me out with this demonic goth project, he would likely be reprimanded.

I got a new job that paid quite poorly but it gave me enough money to move into a very small bedsit near to where I worked. The bedsit had one main room, which had to be my bedroom and living room combined. But I was lucky because my bedsit had its own separate kitchen and bathroom. That meant I didn't need to share either of those with any other tenants in the building. It was warm and cosy unlike the caravan. It was like heaven in my life for a change.

It took a few months to get everything together to prepare my first edition. Meanwhile the drudgery of everyday life of work and not much else tried to grind me down. I may have been free from church and calling myself a Jehovah's Witness, but I was very much living a similar life. I didn't swear, I didn't lie or cheat, I was squeaky clean and honest. My rebellion was still very slow to form past the internal rules of a naïve system. I wanted to be creative in all aspects of my life, so I started to let my hair grow and looked for second-hand clothes that I could be more creative with. I adorned my bedsit with candles and made a huge spider's web out of black wool that covered the whole ceiling in my bedroom / living room. I wrote poetry and constantly listened to music.

I had a small reprieve from the mundane when bumping into someone that would talk to me. One of my former friends in the congregation that now wouldn't have anything to do with me, had a brother Dave, who was no longer a Jehovah's Witness but still lived at home. Sometimes I went to see him if the rest of the family wasn't in the house. Dave introduced me to grown up films. As a Jehovah's Witness I was never allowed to watch any film with a rating greater than PG or 12. Anything with any nudity, swearing or adult themes was simply not allowed. One evening Dave invited me round to the empty house, we got a Chinese takeaway and he hired a video from the video store called The Terminator. I was a child of Star Wars. I was six years old when Star Wars came out. My young life was formed by dreams of space exploration and Princess Leia. But I had never seen anything like the terror of Arny and the super violence of the first Terminator film. It was fantastic!

Dave also took me out to Manchester one night. I had told him about my love for all things gothic and he told me about this amazing club in Manchester that had been around for years called The Banshee. So, he took me along. For some stupid reason I had decided that the course of my life was my own and I was a grown up and could do what I wanted to do, not always because I deeply wanted to, but more because I had the freedom to make up my own mind. Buying a porn mag was something I wanted to do to flex that freedom, but the desire to exercise my free will was more of a decider than the porn. That rebellion got me to start something stupid. I bought cigarettes from the shop and started smoking.

I had only started a couple of weeks before when we went to The Banshee. I thought I was so cool, sitting in a nightclub at a table on my own, dressed all in black, my hair very badly gelled to try and get it to stick up, rebel punk style, Ray-Ban style sunglasses on in the dark of a nightclub, pretending to smoke a cigarette without actually inhaling it and letting it just pour from my mouth like some 40s black and white screen harlot. I must have looked quite a pathetic sight. I thought I looked so cool! The coolness was tested though as the thick white smoke that slowly crept from my lips on nearly every breathe went upwards, up my face, under my plastic sunglasses and straight into my eyes. My eyes smarted and ached and I forced a tear out as I tried so very hard to stay cool and not get a hanky out and smear my basic eyeliner (which no-one could see because of the dark glasses). Strangely, even when I did inhale, smoking never made me cough. If it had, I would have likely stopped as quickly as I started. Instead, like a slippery thief, after a few months I couldn't stop smoking cigarettes. The habit took me without me barely noticing. One day I was just curious and rebellious, then in the space of a couple of months, I didn't want to stop.

-x-

Living in Chesterfield was depressing if you wanted to dress differently. There were no real alternative clothing shops around. The best I could do was try and be creative with what little clothes I could get my hands on. There was one second-hand clothes shop that sold slightly unusual clothes, otherwise department stores and high street fashion shops were the only other choice. I quickly began to realise that men's and women's fashions were completely different in the way they were marketed. The home shopping catalogues that my mum used to shop through always had three quarters of the huge colour catalogue just for women's clothes. What was left was taken up with children's clothes, hardware and toys and then a very small section for men's clothes. This was also reflected in the department stores where most of the floor space was taken up with women's fashion. Then from that limited selection of men's clothes would be just a repetition of the same thing. All the trousers were cut the same but with slightly different shades of brown or navy and then a similar selection in cotton instead of polyester. To be creative with clothing in a backward town in 1991 was practically impossible.

It was then that I started to eye up women's clothes. At first, I had an internal fight with myself about even looking through women's clothes to wear. Surely that would make me a transvestite and if I accepted being a transvestite then I would be open to being homosexual as well? That was my stupid Jehovah's Witness logic, a very simplistic, black and white view of the world and what was evil and what was not.

I came to a stark conclusion.

-x-

What makes a piece of clothing gender in nature? Cotton isn't grown male or female and then different parts used for men's clothes and the other for women's clothes. It's all the same material. I was in town looking through a department store one day and decided to work out what the difference was between a blouse and a man's shirt. I eventually found a woman's blouse that was cut the same as a man's shirt and then compared them. The only difference between the two of them was which side the buttons were on. Who made that decision? If I wore that blouse, would that instantly make me a transvestite and as such, evil in God's eyes? And if that was the result from wearing a piece of cloth that has been designated a gender, is God respecting the authority of the person that decided the gender of a piece of material for Him to be able to make that judgement? How does the person that cuts and designs that material decide on the gender and how do they express it universally? If a dress sits in a store without gender designation, does that allow it to be unisex?

The problem I had with the ridiculousness of it all was, if the gender of a piece of material cannot be defined, then the clothing it is made from cannot be defined. If the gender of a piece of clothing cannot be defined, then a transvestite cannot be sinful, and evil is a stupid notion. In fact, surely the very definition of a transvestite is irrelevant. If I could easily question the morality of accusing a transvestite of being morally wrong and evil than what else could I question? Perhaps even my inbuilt moral ideas of homosexuality were also completely wrong.

What it comes down to eventually is, does what I wear on my body for clothing cause anyone harm? It does not, then all other questions of morality become questionable. This line of thinking made me open my eyes up as to why people wear what they wear. Everyone I had ever known owned a pair of blue jeans. Jeans are made of denim; denim is not naturally blue. So, does everyone love blue? Nope, they wear blue jeans because that is what everyone else wears, that is the norm, that is accepted, like the gender of clothes. Jeans can be dyed any colour and yet the vast majority of jeans that are bought are blue. I was never going to buy a pair of blue jeans ever again.

From then on, I was wearing what I liked and what creatively worked for me, regardless of the expectation of that clothing.

# 4

## AUTUMN 1991, 20 YEARS OLD

My hair was growing wild, my clothes were getting more unusual, I was turning into a poseur with my pathetic way of smoking without inhaling. A few months ago, I had bumped into one of Dave's neighbours called Sam and we went out for a drink in the village I lived in. I wasn't used to drinking at all. I had only been partially drunk once in my life. The only pubs I ever used to go to as a Jehovah's Witness were country pubs when either we had been out for a walk for the day or gone out for a meal somewhere. I was brought up to believe that the local pubs were dens of debauchery, filth and drunkenness, places to steer clear of under any circumstance. Local pubs still made me nervous.

As soon as Sam and I entered the local village pub, I stood out like a sore thumb, dressed in tight black jeans with three buckle belts around my waist and a white pirate shirt, smoking my cigarettes like a porn star (I thought, although how I would know...?). I was very aware that I had a target on me because I looked different. I may as well have had a neon flashing light in pink following me around with an arrow pointing down at my head, spelling out 'kill the queer.' I only drank a couple of pints of bitter. Sam was quite a big guy, and he knew how to look after himself, so for a while I felt quite safe in his company. But as the evening went on, there was quite a large group of kids congregating outside the pub with a couple of them starting to make their way inside. They made a beeline for me. They were young thugs laughing at me and asking for a cigarette off me. I gave one of them a cigarette and then decided to pre-empt any trouble and leave and make for home about a mile away.

As Sam and I got outside we were faced with the crowd of kids which was huge. There were more than 30 of them ranging from around 12 years old to about 16, hanging around in the dark about 11 o'clock on a Saturday night. All of them thought I was a comedy piece, existing for their entertainment. I looked to Sam for support and the fresh air had doubled the effect of the evening's drinking on him and all of a sudden, he looked completely drunk. Sam made a passing attempt to try and thump a couple of the older lads which scattered them across the car park. I took the lead in making our way onto the main road and home.

As we walked down the road away from the pub,

Sam just got more and more drunk as the cool evening air ran through his lungs. In the distance the kids were shouting abuse and throwing missiles down the road towards us which landed very short. They covered the whole way across the main road, there were that many of them, like a riot making its way down the street. I started to feel a little at ease as the distance increased and we were nearly out of sight when Sam declared drunkenly, "where's my coat?" I looked back in the direction of the kids still shouting abuse at the top of their voices and lying on the road halfway back to the pub was Sam's coat.

Part of me decided to just let it go and leave his coat where it lay. A shiver of fear ran down my spine. I knew that walking back towards those thugs, still throwing missiles in our direction, would be seen as an act of defiance against them and could easily trigger something worse. There was a chance though that Sam had something in one of his coat pockets that he didn't want to lose like his wallet or driving licence. I had no choice, I left him drunkenly wobbling in the street and I marched back towards the crowd. I had to wonder where all the parents of those children were and why they didn't care where their own kids were and what they were doing so late on a Saturday night. The volume of the crowd had just started to dissipate a little and some kids had started to wander off until one of them saw me walking back towards them. As expected, it just re-focused all of them and they all bunched back up and started to walk towards me.

At first, they matched my steps as I got closer to the coat on the floor, but as I got closer the gang started to pick up in volume again and rocks and stones where hurling through the air in my direction.

I grabbed the coat as casually as I could and turned to walk back to Sam who had disappeared around the corner. Behind me I could hear the footsteps quickening faster than mine until panic got the better of me and I looked around to see the sea of kids running headlong down the middle of the main road, screaming abuse and violent intention. It was a sight I thought I would never see.

The panic grabbed hold of me and I started to quicken my walk into a run. As I caught up with Sam, I shouted to him to start running, but he was so drunk that he could hardly walk. There was a light, like a beacon of hope lighting up the street just a couple of hundred yards away. It was the local fish and chip shop with the door open and offering refuge within. I motioned to Sam to run for the shop, but he decided that escape lay in a parked car instead and proceeded to get on all fours and crawl under the car.

I ran into the chip shop and asked the manager to call the police. Once he saw the riotous, shouting throng of teenagers running menacingly towards his shop he agreed to call the police but insisted that I wait outside. In a panic the shop owner came around the counter and ushered me outside and then shut the door behind him leaving me defenceless against the growing number of rowdy kids running up to the shop front. I stood there facing them, so scared I wanted to cry out. I was very concerned about Sam. I could see him underneath the car and because the whole focus was on me, all the kids ran straight past him not noticing. He was relatively safe if they all drew to me. I thought to run home, but I didn't want to leave Sam and I certainly didn't want them all knowing where I lived. A couple of the ring leaders came up to me, giving me abuse to my face. All the kids were jumping up and down and shouting encouragement to the ring leaders to beat me up and fuck me over.

I could see Sam starting to crawl out from under the car and a few lads saw him and started to make their way over towards him. I shouted out that they all needed to go home as the police were on their way. That just got the crowd going again and the kids moved away from the car and back to me. There were so many of them. One of the leaders started to punch me about the face. I've been hit around the head so many times in my life that its nothing surprising. I was knocked unconsciousness once in the playground of the secondary school. Being a Jehovah's Witness was always very tough at school. I was used to being punched.

All I could think about was not retaliating. There were so many of them that I didn't stand a chance if they all decided to join in and beat me up. I knew the police were on their way and all I could think about were the consequences of smashing a young lads head against the wall just as the police turn up. That would be it for me, my life would be over. Being charged with beating up a child and getting sent to prison. I knew that in an ideal world I could say that I was protecting myself, but the legal system has never fully defended the innocent, I was very aware of that. I needed to get through this without any long-term consequences.

The leader of the gang shouted and spat abuse in my face and punched me a couple more times. It was almost like being in the firing line of one of my mum's uncontrolled temper tantrums.

It didn't take long for them to realise that I wasn't going to retaliate and for some reason the few thugs leading the charge didn't know how to react to that. The physical violence stopped and they just turned back to verbal abuse. The leader spitting abuse in my face only looked about 15 years old and thankfully there wasn't much power behind his punches. He backed off, obviously bored already that the whole situation wasn't going anywhere. Slowly, the whole crowd backed off. The verbal abuse started to lessen as the kids got bored that nothing was happening and the whole situation just seemed to fizzle out like the little spits and spats at the end of a dying fireworks sparkler.

As the crowd dispersed, I wanted to stay where I was. I had asked the shop keeper to call the police and when the police arrived, I planned to explain the situation and give descriptions of the young leaders of the gang. But I quickly realised that Sam had gone, he had disappeared, and I hadn't seen where he had gone. I left my home address and name with the shop keeper to hand over to the police, if they ever turned up, and set off nervously to try and find Sam. I quickly walked around part of the village, shaking with fear that the riotous gang may have regrouped somewhere else and that I would accidently find them around a corner of a street and the whole thing would kick off again. I felt so scared, alone and exposed in my marginally unusual clothes. That town was so culturally primitive.

After a frantic search for 15 minutes around the immediate area, I decided the most likely place he would go would be back at the bedsit where he had also parked his car, so I rushed back there. When I got home, Sam's car was still there, but there was no sign of him at all. My bedsit was in the middle of a building of apartments. I worried that if he returned, he may struggle to get into the building to get to the bedsit, so I sat outside on the street, watching for a sign of Sam anywhere, all the while fearing that at some point the large crowd of thugs might come down the road looking for me. After an anxious half hour wait, a police car finally arrived. I gave the two policeman a run-down of what had happened, brief descriptions of the young lads, who the police seemed to know the identity of straight away. They asked if I wanted to press charges against them. I thought that if you broke the law, you got arrested. Why was it up to me to decide if they should be arrested? I had no real bruises on me, I knew in the end it would be my word against 30 kids' versions of reality.

My concern became where Sam was. I explained to the police that I was very worried about him as he was very drunk when I lost him. I was concerned that he might have fallen drunkenly into a ditch and passed out wearing only a t-shirt and a pair of trousers. The night was very cool and I had fears of him dying of exposure in some industrial wasteland. My imagination had always been prone to over dramatization! The police said they would do a search of the village to try and find him. They really didn't seem to care much at all and went on their way, leaving me in the street way past midnight waiting for Sam to return.

After another anxious half hour, a small figure appeared walking down the street. It was the 15 year old leader of the gang, the one that snarled and spat in my face and punched me a few times. Now the tables were turned. It was him and me and no-one around in the middle of the night. I faced up to him and stood in his path and politely told him that I was now ready to take up that argument that we never finished. The coward started bumbling, fidgeting and started to pretend that his dad was walking down the street behind me. He was such a coward, and he ran as fast as he could doing a 20-yard circle around me, running off into the night like the child that he was.

Sam never came back to the bedsit that night.

When I eventually went to bed and awoke the next morning, his car was still parked outside. Sometime later that day, he drove the car away without calling on me and letting me know he was ok. It was another couple of weeks before I saw him again. He was really pissed off with me for not fighting off the kids that were trying to get under the car at him. He was absolutely fine, didn't have a scratch on him. None of the kids had even touched him and when he got out from under the car, he went straight to a relative's home nearby in the same village and stayed there for the night. I was relieved that he was ok, but annoyed that he lay blame on me. For me it was the best outcome that could possibly have come from the whole scenario. I came away with an intense fear of the village at night. I had no desire to go back to that pub. Every dark night I would try and not venture out from my bedsit at all.

A few weeks later, I did venture nervously to the Chinese takeaway one night for a rare treat. Two young men in their early twenties were walking by the shop window as I was waiting for my food order and they did a double take when they saw me. Instead of walking the path they were on, they said something to each other and marched into the takeaway, straight up to me thumped me in the head and knocked me to the floor, then kicked me a few times while I lay curled up on the floor.

"You threatened to beat up my younger brother you fucking queer. If I see you anywhere again, I'll kill you!" shouted the knuckle dragging neanderthal.

The girl behind the counter had screamed and the father came out from the back room and started shouting at them to leave. After a few racist calls to the takeaway owners, the two monsters left and carried on walking down the street.

The owner of the takeaway was very sweet. They wanted to call the police, but I said there was no point. I took my food home and tried to eat my dinner instead of throwing up.

Sam eventually made a partial truce with me and drove me out into the countryside for a drink at a nice quiet country pub. I told him how I had done what I thought was best that night. He was still angry with me regardless. I thought that we were very lucky. Neither of us came out scarred or with anything that could ruin our lives. Once again, compared with death itself, the monster I had faced, this was nothing really. Both of us spent the evening at the country pub mourning being single, stuck in dead end jobs and being alone for the rest of our lives. Sam did say with total conviction that he thought it was highly likely that I would meet some lovely goth girl and live happily ever after. I laughed at him, that seemed such a far off and impossible notion.

The spectre of fear continued to follow me every time I ventured out in the evening, especially locally. The walk to work when on the night shift was always one of fear. The walk home in the morning was easier as I knew that thugs weren't awake at six in the morning.

-x-

My long-term plan was in place. My fanzine would be put together using paper, scissors and glue, which would create a master that I could get photocopied and then sell somehow. I just needed some content and bit more experience of my subject, the gothic genre.

I worked at a factory in the village, a small unit with just a handful of employees. The work was repetitive, tedious, boring and very low paid. The money I earned was barely enough to pay for my rent, food, utilities and have enough left over to fund my new project. During the day there was little opportunity to talk to anyone. The noise of the machines being spread yards away from each other meant that most of the working day was spent doing repetitive tasks. Each shift had a base number of the same task that are achievable within the shift period. That number was based on what the guys who were already there before I began working there had established as achievable in a shift period. During a normal day, with the usual distractions, those targets were ok and we made sure we kept to those numbers.

Then we started to do shifts.

Although initially I hated the thought of doing a nightshift, a couple of weeks into doing them I found that it suited me quite well. I had a shift supervisor called Caleb. He had been a student at college for a couple of years in the eighties and was heavily into the alternative music scene. We got on really well. We both found that we could work hard for about three hours and get nearly our entire quota of work done and then have the rest of the night free to do what we wanted. When both of us first worked that out, I was very uncomfortable with it. But Caleb convinced me that they paid me a set fee and wouldn't pay me any more for producing two or three times the amount even if I did.

Caleb would bring his record player into work and all of his vinyl records. He introduced me to quite a few amazing goth bands that were in my Gothic Rock book but I hadn't listened to before. I immediately caught onto a band called Danse Society and would ask Caleb to play those singles all the time. He also introduced me to The Virgin Prunes and Sex Gang Children, music that blew me away it was so amazing. Goth music from the eighties was so diverse and so different. I would talk for hours with Caleb about goth music. He had known two tribes of goths at college. There were serious, stuck up ones that were very elitist and then a bunch that were more punk in their attitude and were very open and fun. I knew which type I preferred to be.

Caleb explained to me how goth had come out of the punk movement of the seventies. How it took a DIY ethos from punk and a belief that anyone can be anything they want to be. If there wasn't an infrastructure to support what you needed, you went and did it yourself. It became very apparent that initially goth punk had caused an explosion in music styles and experimentation, but by the end of the eighties, goth music was narrowing its scope. It had now become so narrow it was defined mostly by a small group of rock bands that played a very similar style of music to each other.

Part of me was disappointed that I had missed the boat, that I was at the end of a movement struggling for existence and losing its scope. I still held out hope of meeting some of those that believed in that dark and deep romanticism. I wanted to belong to a new tribe, a tribe that believed in a deep love and an appreciation for a dark art. I wanted to belong to a culture that questioned the norm and questioned why everything around us is the way it is and if things when scrutinised look silly and stupid, throwing away those rules and living free of them. I had escaped Jehovah's Witnesses and their control, I also wanted to escape society and its control.

But I still had common sense obstacles.

Embarrassingly the manager of the factory took me to one side and had to tell me that I was starting to smell quite badly. My life was being lived between work and home, home and work. When I washed my clothes, they dried inside the bedsit. None of my clothes breathed as my bedsit had no air. It was so embarrassing to be confronted by such a truth, but I'm glad I was, before I started fully mixing with the outside world. I didn't know how to change it though. It wasn't my body that smelled, it was the stale air of the bedsit. That discussion prompted Caleb to tell me about the magic of incense. To me the burning of incense was purely a religious practice, something Jehovah's Witnesses never did because of the connection to Catholic churches or paganism.

Caleb told me about how incense was actually an air deodoriser and cleaner, probably used by the churches to hide the smell of the peasants. So, I started to buy huge amounts of incense really cheaply and constantly burned them ten at a time. I haven't had a problem with smelling bad since. Once again that proved to me that not questioning rules and taboos actually worked against me. I really needed to get rid of all my preconceptions, whether moral, religious or ones imposed by society, after all that was part of being a goth.

One of the bands based in Sheffield from the Gothic Rock book wrote back to me and accepted an interview. So now I was armed and ready to travel all the way to Sheffield to do an interview with a bunch of very strange people I'd never met, about a topic I was not quite sure about, at a place I'd never been to before, on public transport that I hardly ever used! And to do that I would have to walk through the village at night on my own dressed up in my weird clothes. Every part of this plan was frightening the hell out of me, but next to the spectre of death, it was nothing. None of it would kill me.

## 5

## WINTER 1991 / 92
## 21 YEARS OLD

My confidence was finally starting to push through. I had worked hard to get over my fears and the many anxious obstacles to reach this point.

That first interview I conducted in Sheffield was the first of many steps to overcome my fears. I managed to get a bus into town, a train to Sheffield, buy two pints at the pub, and get the same transport back home all from a ten-pound note. I also got back home in time to go straight to work and do my night shift with Caleb.

I interviewed a band called Autumn of North. I was so pleased with myself that I had overcome my fear of travelling to a place I didn't know. I found the pub in Sheffield easily enough. The hardest part of the evening was walking into the pub, having no idea what it would be like in there and then wondering how I was going to find out who my contact was. It was absolutely fine of course. I got a drink from the bar and watched as a band set up their instruments in one corner ready to play. There was hardly any audience there at all, so it was obvious that everyone knew each other and I must have stuck out like a sore thumb. My contact was a young lad called Tim Chandler and he noticed me on my own and made a beeline for me and introduced himself. He was so polite and lovely and asked me to sit tight as they were just about to go on and play.

So I had a chance to relax while I watch the band play their set. Afterwards Tim arranged for the whole band to sit in a side room to let me interview them all. The interview was the most difficult part. I had a load of questions ready for them, but they were very playful, a little drunk and they were too busy jumping around the room, laughing and joking that the interview just descended into chaos. It was a good lesson in many ways. The recording wasn't very clear as there was too much happening in the room. I did manage to get some things out of the interview to do a piece for my fanzine. Most of all I learned how nice people are and that I had little to fear really.

I didn't get beaten up in the village on the way home, I didn't get lost on the public transport and the band didn't rob me or try and covert me to worshipping the devil and make animal sacrifices. So all in all, it was a very pleasant and successful evening.

I quickly learned the complexities of doing a fanzine. To make the master, I had to plan out the flat sheets first. So the cover, inside cover, back and inside back were all on one sheet, then pages 2, 3 and 18, 19 of a twenty page fanzine then needed to be done next. Making the pages up was done by typing text out on my typewriter on a piece of paper, then cutting that piece out to the shape I wanted and pasting it to the master. I also had the photographs that I took at gigs developed at a shop then pasted into the masters. Then I had pieces of artwork and décor, drawn borders etc cut out and glued to the masters.

Then, when the masters were ready, I would call Ivan and he would pick me up in his car and take me to his factory either in an evening or at the weekend when no-one was around. He would charge me for the photocopying, but not the petrol for travelling all the way to his factory and back. He was so very sweet to do that. I would make about 50 copies of every master, take them home and then painstakingly staple them together. It was all very DIY and I became very proud of having that achievement of 50 fanzines laid out completed in front of me, even if the content wasn't that great really.

I originally called my fanzine Black Death. It was a reflection of my rebirth after taking those nine pills. According to my family and all my former friends I was evil and damned. It seemed a very apt description of where the content was coming from.

I soon found out that two bands I was in touch with were playing at a nightclub on the same night and at the same venue in Sheffield. They were called Empyrean and Nosferatu. I got in touch with them and arranged to meet them for interviews. They were playing on a Saturday night and the club didn't open until 9pm. The chances of me catching the last train home that evening would be very slim, but I was a man without fear and it was a great chance to get two interviews done in one night. On the day, I dressed up and decided to try and find the venue in the daytime while I could read a map in the daylight with the idea of then going to a pub for a few hours and going back later in the evening when the venue opened. I found the venue around 3pm and to my surprise a hearse was parked outside. Out of the hearse got these three tall men with huge heads of backcombed and crimped black hair and frilly shirts. It was the band Nosferatu. I introduced myself and they let me into the club with them as they hauled their gear into the venue.

I had never seen inside a nightclub before in the daylight. It was very strange. The walls were all very badly painted in matt black that looked awful in daylight with bits of tape and flaking plaster coming off the walls. It was a real eyeopener for how fake the industry obviously is, especially when the stage was noticeably just a load of tables pushed and taped together. When the doors were shut and the daylight was gone, the illusion was returned to an atmospheric place of dreams.

It was interesting to watch the whole process of an evening in a nightclub. The sound system being set up and the sound checks. Sound checks were generally done in reverse order, so the headline act did their sound check first, then the support band did theirs after. That way when the first band go on, all their levels are already set and ready to go. Empyrean were the support band for the night, but they didn't turn up until 6pm some three hours after the headline act Nosferatu had arrived.

That did mean that Nosferatu could get their soundcheck done very early, before the other band had even turned up. It was great to be there and be able to take a load of photos of them on stage with no audience and be able to move around the place and use different angles to get them captured without restriction.

There was quite a difference between the two bands. Nosferatu were a three piece with a drum machine. They were very clean, very well presented and obviously not short of a bob or two. They had very beautifully presented, sharp frilly and velvety clothes like some strange Victorian horror fantasy. They had just released a 12" vinyl single on their own label. They had their own fanzine called Grimoire that was perfect in its design, all done on computer and quality printed. Everything smacked of money, including their instruments and accents. Empyrean on the other hand were a bunch of common scruffs, covered in old biker leathers, biker boots and messy hair. They talked and acted working class and it was easy for me to relate to them and look on detached and admiringly at Nosferatu. From the banter between the two bands though it was obvious that Nosferatu were overconfident and were easily wound up by the working-class lads. Also, Nosferatu came almost on their own and yet Empyrean had an entourage with them.

With Nosferatu finished with their set up and soundcheck and Empyrean just starting to pull their gear into the venue, I asked Nosferatu if I could interview them in a side room. I managed to find another bar room which had some comfy chairs and was away from the noise of the main nightclub being set up. Only two of the three band members came in to talk to me. I didn't ask where the guitarist was. The bass player called himself Vlad Janicek and the singer went by the name Louis DeWray. Before we even started, I asked if they would sign my copy of the 12" EP that I had taken along with me, which they kindly did.

I started my tape recorder placed on the table between us and I proceeded with the interview. Both were really accommodating. All of my questions were around being goth, what that meant to them, how it influenced them, if they had an issue with that term, all those kinds of questions. Vlad had quite a bit to say instead of just single word answers, so the interview was very smooth but very serious, they were serious musicians.

At the end I asked Vlad how many interviews they had done, and apparently, I was one of the first magazines / fanzines to interview them, which filled me with great pride. As Vlad got up to leave the room, Louis shared a bit of a laugh and a joke, so I took the opportunity to ask him how he got his hair to stick up the way it did. I had been using hair gels and hairsprays for a year or so, but I just couldn't get my hair to defy gravity and do what I wanted it to do.

He reached to his back pocket and got out a comb. "You have to backcomb it," he said moving towards me with the comb in his hand like a weapon. "First you need to crimp your hair, that puts the strength into it, then you have to backcomb it like this.." and he grabbed a piece of my hair on the top of my head, pulled it up vertically, then got the comb and used it downwards towards my head. "There you go," he said standing back and admiring his handywork. "You have to make sure you use a comb; a brush doesn't work very well." I moved across the room to see my reflection in the mirrors behind the bar while Louis laughed heartily. That strip of hair on the top of my head, without any hairspray or gel applied stood vertically up on my head. It was a revelation!

The interview had gone really well and gave me quite the confidence boost to move onto interviewing Empyrean. The members of Empyrean had finished their sound check so they were free to do their interview. They all piled into the back room with me and I got them all settled. In a similar way to the Autumn of North interview I had done some weeks before, Empyrean were a bunch of lads that liked to mess around a little, but I managed to keep them focused a little more. They weren't as happy as Nosferatu were with my line of questioning. They didn't really see themselves as a goth band, more of a heavy rock band, so all the questions about the goth culture became quite irrelevant.

-x-

It was a strange time in music history. The majority of bands that would be called gothic, totally denied having anything to do with the name tag. All the bands hated it and would publicly ridicule anyone calling them by that name. The Sisters of Mercy had a massive goth following, but they hated goths and at every opportunity would say that publicly. It was so strange to live in a time when bands publicly offended and threw hatred to their own fanbase. Nosferatu were actually proud to be called goth, Empyrean were not and hated the term, even though they were playing at a goth venue supporting a proudly gothic band.

Bands hated the term simply because the press took the piss out of goth all the time. There was a stereotype of goths being miserable and depressed, moping and moaning all the time. Much of the music is depressing and morbid, full of misery and depression, but for some people like myself, that is what life was like, that is what reflected back at me. My life wasn't parties, fun and escapism. Being a former Jehovah's Witness did teach me a few things. One valuable lesson was that escapism doesn't solve anything at all and shouldn't be used as a way of life, because when the escape stops, the problems are still there. When you get drunk, take drugs, or just spend all your time partying, or always listening to escapist happy music or watching films to escape all the time and purely entertain, the problems you escape from are still there and, if you carry on ignoring them will probably get worse. Facing up to problems is the first step to trying to do something about them. Even now, having films, music and art that reflect my problems and dark feelings, helps me face mine and take comfort in art's understanding of me.

All things in moderation.

I always thought that goth stereotypes were like most stereotypes, very lazy and short-sighted and I couldn't help but be annoyed by bands that encouraged that stereotype.

-x-

The interview with Empyrean finished. It was ok, it wasn't as engaging as the one with Nosferatu, but Vlad and Louis from Nosferatu were very sure of themselves and were very serious about their art, almost boringly so. At least Empyrean were a bit more down to earth and had a good laugh.

I hung around with Empyrean for the rest of the evening. The drummer, Mark Haines, spent a lot of time doodling, it was a way for him to concentrate while having a conversation, a habit I picked up from him since. His drawings were amazing. He spent the evening doing a couple of covers for me for the next couple of issues of my fanzines. We got on really well.

It was an evening like no other I had experienced so far in my short life. I had gone out with plenty of fear and anxiety. I had a plan of how the day was going to go and even though the day was not as planned, I still came through with two great interviews and the experience of an interesting day. It was so good that when the night finished about one in the morning, I didn't want to go home. I enjoyed the company I was with, I was quietly proud of myself, but I didn't want to go back to very dull and lonely bedsit miles away. I did have some disappointment. I had hoped to meet loads of really interesting goths, hoped to have seen many gorgeous and beautiful people but in actuality there weren't many people that turned up for the gig, the venue was barely half full and the promise of beauty I had seen inside the pages of the Gothic Rock book wasn't there. I was starting to believe that this was a culture on the wane. Gone were the huge hair, punk attitude, deep romanticism and beauty to die for and in comes the rock crowd, flat crimped hair and velvet lines of kids, one following the style of the other instead of wild uncontrolled creativity. But still, this was my new tribe and I still hoped to be able to find my kin.

When the lights in the nightclub went up just after 1am, I had already missed my train back home. The plan was to wait until the first coach or train back home the next morning which would be about 7am on the next day, Sunday. This was the new me. I had no idea what a country village boy was going to do for six hours in a strange city in the middle of the night.

I needed to delay the inevitable and spend as little time on my own as possible, in the dark, in the cold and in fear in a strange city centre. It took the club owners about an hour to empty the nightclub and go home, then the two bands had to take out all their gear and load it into the various pieces of transport. I couldn't believe that after such a long day and so late at night, the bands were still going to drive all the way home for a few hours more instead of staying at a hotel. I was so naive when it came to the nuts and bolts of gigging. Nosferatu were packed and gone by 2am, Empyrean had parked their van miles away, so it took ages for someone to go and fetch it. We all sat outside the venue for ages chatting and laughing away like we all had nowhere to go and no cares in the world.

I didn't want the chatting to end. The thought of what I could possibly do for a few hours in the middle of a frightening city on my own at night made me very nervous. I started to probe the band members to see if their journey back took them down the M1 motorway anywhere near where I lived. Walking a few miles in familiar territory was preferable to waiting around the city centre. I don't know what it was I feared. If you were a person that was likely to rob a person at knife point, you probably wouldn't hang around a very quiet city centre hoping to bump into someone with money. I had no money anyway, so I had nothing to steal, except for a £100 camera perhaps.

Empyrean were on a different path home and weren't going in my direction. So, I just tried to keep the conversation going for as long as possible to minimise the exposure time in the city until the first transport home.

It was just passed 3am by the time everything was packed into the van and we all said our goodbyes. I was sad to see them go. It had been an evening of highs and fears challenged and suddenly in the space of just a few minutes, I was alone again, facing a massive fear and for the first time I could feel the morning cold starting to bite into my skin.

I walked into the very centre of the city and looked for somewhere sheltered, safe and warm to spend the next four hours. I found that a coach would be available in the morning before the trains. The first coach was just after 7am. I could waste half an hour finding some breakfast if anything would be open first thing on a Sunday morning, so I only needed to hang around for just two and a half hours. The coach and bus station had closed its doors by the time I got to the building. I walked down to the train station and that was also all closed and barriered off for the night. I was very tired and starting to get cold. My leather jacket was very thick and heavy, but not very warm at all.

After walking around for half an hour looking for somewhere to stay, the only place I could find were the many bus shelters near the coach station. There were a couple of homeless people that had taken the best spots nearer to the station shutters which looked cosy and sheltered. I thought it best to perhaps stay away from anyone else just in case a fight between the homeless guys kicked off. I don't know why I thought that, I just wanted to minimise any risk at all. So I picked a spot that was shielded from the direction of the very cold breeze. Once I got settled there was still freezing air circulating around me. My leather jacket was a useless blanket. For all my preparation for the gig, I hadn't really done any preparation for sleeping rough. A blanket, a small pillow, even a decent woolly jumper would have been a good idea, but I hadn't packed any of those things. I had cigarettes. What an idiot!

The wire mesh plastic seats in the glass bus shelter were extremely uncomfortable. The way they were shaped, to fit a large person's bottom, did not help when you want to spread yourself across three of them to attempt to, at the very least, lie down. But the ridges and bumps made it impossible. With each passing minute my mood descended and sunk deep down. From such a high I was slipping down so very fast into a dark and really cold place. I started to hope that someone may try and rob me and stab me and put me out of my misery. My imagination went off on a journey of being found dead clutching the cassette tape of the two interviews I had done and the photos on my camera. "Maybe one of the bands might do a dedication song for me," was where my fantasy took me.

It didn't take long for the cold morning air to start to work its way into my bones. I had slept rough a couple of times and it was the most awful experience. It was quite a warm night, but the morning air, just into double figures on the thermometer, wrapped itself around me plunging me into a bitter shiver. Then just half an hour in, the cold penetrated every layer of clothing and through the top layer of my skin. It crept into my sublayers, into my muscle and fat and then eventually I could feel my very bones getting cold. I looked at my watch, it was not even 4am. I was so cold and so tired and so very down and alone.

I tried to close my eyes and sleep, but it was difficult when so cold. Every noise for half a mile in each direction made me jolt with fear and I would have to open my eyes and look to check if I was safe. I was pretty much blocked into the shelter. If anyone decided to have a go at me, I didn't really have a clear escape route. I clung to my rucksack containing the cassette recorder, empty sandwich box and camera. I had worked hard for the contents of my bag and I was not going to let anyone steal it.

Time seemed to stop. Every minute felt like an age. I got so tired that I resigned myself eventually to just let whatever happens to me happen. The noises became less startling, and I fell into a semi-state of consciousness where I was aware of everything around me, but I had stiffened my limbs into a part sleep state, still penetrated by cold. I had a word with myself. At least I had a home and a job to go back to in a few hours. I had food and warmth there. I was in the midst of people that had none of those things to look forward to. I was actually very rich. A home, food, a little money, a job. As much as I didn't like my job or bedsit or being alone, I still had a life of plenty in relation to the homeless guys sheltering in the station.

# 6

## SUMMER 1992, 21 YEARS OLD

Going back to work on a Monday morning always sent my levels back to the bottom again. I really didn't like my workplace. The work was repetitive and very boring and most of the staff were either self-obsessed, immoral idiots or just really dull individuals that thought they led exciting lives.

I've always been a person that tries to get as much out of life as I can. I try and appreciate every little thing. I love the beauty of the countryside where I live. There is so much beauty everywhere and in everything. I know that I am both blessed and cursed. I have a heart that is so constantly overwhelmed with love and emotion. Everywhere has beauty if you care to look for it. But I'm also easily heartbroken and constantly disappointed with people and the world. I didn't find any real love or warmth or affection in the Jehovah's Witnesses and it seems to be just as scarce in the real world as well. Nearly all my work colleagues are without any love and affection at all, in fact they seem scared and offended by the idea.

The production of my fanzines ran smoothly enough. I called myself the Black Angel as the Author. I had no interest in my real name, it meant nothing at all to me. My former self died of nine pills in the caravan. My family didn't seem to be that bothered about me, so my name had no relevance. The name Black Angel would do for the time being. It summed me up. Fallen, tarnished, banished, dark and yet I did have beauty, I was a good person, I was caring, I felt and loved intensely and deeply just without focus.

I regularly put advertisements in the back page section of the NME, a national music newspaper. It was quite reasonably priced for a national paper. People sent me money sellotaped to a piece of card with their mailing address and in return I posted them a copy of the fanzine. The first copy featured the Autumn of North interview. The second had the Nosferatu interview and had Mark Haines' artwork on the front. I asked my fanzine readers from around the country to send in pieces of poetry and artwork to put in future issues. I also had a section for folk to send in requests for pen pals. That was so people can strike up friendships by writing letters to each other through the post. I purposefully added this section so that I could find people to write to.

-x-

I was always hoping I would meet someone special. The words of my friend Sam where always running through my head. I couldn't understand why Sam was so sure that I would meet some 'nice goth girl' when I couldn't stop thinking that I would live a life on my own.

Quite by accident one day, I bumped into an old school friend called Andy. Andy and I had been best friends at school which was unusual because I wasn't really allowed to have friends outside the congregation. Outside or 'worldly' friends were seen as a bad influence by Jehovah's Witnesses, so contact with any should be kept to a minimum. Bumping into Andy now that I wasn't a Jehovah's Witness made me realise a few things. For some reason Andy wasn't classed as a bad influence, in fact it's only in looking back that I realise that my mum didn't take any notice of who I was hanging around with outside of school, as though she didn't actually care. Most of my paranoia about friends that were worldly was self-regulated, which is a bizarre concept to realise.

There was an embarrassing period at the end of school when I decided that to become a good Jehovah's Witness I had to try and at least convert any worldly people I knew. So, I tried to start a Bible study with Andy. It was a strange thing to do. I think I did it partly as a subconscious way to work out 'the truth' for myself. I had all those questions of theology that just didn't make any sense and damaged my faith, but no-one would give me answers to and yet I had a firm belief in some scientific and historical facts that were absolutes and proved the Bible. I think that studying with Andy was a way for me to work out the logic in my own head as well. It didn't last very long, Andy's mum got word of the Bible study and stopped it in its tracks.

It had been a few years after leaving school that I bumped into Andy randomly on the street. He had been to sixth form and then onto university in Leeds, while I was stuck in a bedsit and working in a plastics factory. Andy was nearly finished at university and asked me if I wanted to stay at his student shared house for a couple of days for a short holiday. I snapped up the opportunity as visiting a strange city was easy for the new me now.

Leeds had become a self-promoted city of goth for some reason in the early nineties. The Sisters of Mercy, supposedly the biggest goth band in the world, were proudly from Leeds. I think it was the NME that painted that picture of Leeds as goth central. So, I had to go and explore, especially the night life.

I took Andy up on his offer and forced myself to go to Leeds on a coach. I had got myself so nervous and anxious on the day, that I was throwing up in the coach's toilet for nearly quarter of an hour and nearly missed the Leeds stop. Although I was determined to break out and create myself a new life, the fear still had a hold and would regularly still make me ill from anxiety. I was not going to let it stop me doing anything though. Next to the spectre of death, nothing was anywhere near as scary.

It was great to spend time with Andy and get away from my bedsit. It really seemed that Andy was living this other life that I was only privileged to glimpse. The shared house he lived in with a bunch of other students was less glamourous than my bedsit in the coldness of reality. We spent a day shopping in the city. For a whole day I dragged Andy around a city he had no interest in. I found an amazing goth clothes shop and bought some great winkle picker boots with loads of buckles on them. Those boots were so goth. I also found some fantastic second-hand record shops and bought an album by Xmal Deutschland (another band on the 4AD label) and also an album by Diamanda Galas called The Plague Mass. Diamanda Galas is another extreme of the goth genre. Amazing, very frightening, horrific and poignant music that from the moment I discovered her, had a heavy influence on me.

I couldn't visit Leeds, the city of all things goth, without going to a goth nightclub. While I was shopping I asked around for what clubs were running on a Saturday night that were goth themed. To my surprise there weren't any at all. The only alternative nightclub that ran on a Saturday night was called Le Phonographique. It was a general alternative nightclub that might sometimes play some goth stuff. I still had to go though, if there were tons of goths in the area they would have to go somewhere. Unfortunately, Andy wasn't at all interested in clubs or the Leeds nightlife and did not want to go out at all. So I plucked up my courage and went out on my own.

Going to a nightclub in a strange city where I don't know a single soul was one of the hardest things I did. I know what I must have looked like, sat there on my own with a single pint of bitter in my strange little 'pretending to be goth' outfit and my uncomfortably new goth winkle pickers. I sat there, chain smoking, trying to stretch out the pint in front of me for as long as possible. I still hadn't been properly drunk yet in my life. I didn't want to ever lose control or give my former family and friends in the congregation the satisfaction of becoming what they predicted, a worldly useless drunk drug taker, a man without any moral compass. I had a fear of getting drunk, even more so in a strange place where I thought I really needed my wits about me.

I had been to a couple of nightclubs before. Sam had once taken me to a nightclub in my local town. The nightclub was called the Adam and Eve. I remember the reputation it had when I was a Jehovah's Witness. Whenever we went passed the building, someone would say, "that's where the most immoral behaviour happens, it's like a sex orgy nearly every night in there, tut, tut." I always wondered that if Jehovah's Witnesses aren't allowed in nightclubs and if they don't associate with people of the outside world, how do they know so much about a local nightclub and what happens in it? The night Sam took me to the Adam and Eve was a Tuesday night, known as the 'grab a Granny' night. It was an evening supposedly where you couldn't fail to get sex because it was full of older divorcee's trying to reclaim a missed youth. It was all a load of rubbish. There was hardly anyone there at all, the women that were there didn't have any interest in a pair of sad loners like Sam and me. By midnight we were bored and had gone home.

So, I sat there on my own in the Leeds club, Le Phonographique, looking very sheepish and pathetic, full of fear and nervousness, with my pint and pack of cigarettes, hoping that someone would talk to me because I didn't have the nerve to strike up a conversation with any stranger in the club.

A large group of students parked themselves next to me along the bench that stretched along an entire wall of the nightclub. There were so many of them that they started to bump into me on the edge of their group. Most of them were already quite tipsy and acting silly. In the centre of their group was a very confident young woman that was the obvious centre of the whole group. She was in her mid-twenties and was with her boyfriend who seemed very fed up and extremely drunk or stoned. After only 15 minutes or so of being bumped into several times and of drunken 'sorry's being thrown towards me, the young woman saw me, told me that I should not be sitting there all on my own and instructed me to sit in the middle of the group next to her. She was such a bubbly, confident and wild thing, I was instantly smitten with her, but I was constantly aware of her miserable boyfriend and the repercussions that could come from even the slightest sign of flirting on my part, intentional or not.

I got drawn into conversations about what music I liked, where I was from, why I was in Leeds, questions about my fanzine and then I got dragged onto the dancefloor when the Sisters of Mercy got played. I had never danced in front of others before and was so self-conscious, but everyone else was drunk, so I could tell no-one cared how stupid I looked.

As the night drew on, another girl started up a more personal conversation. We talked for a couple of hours and I really liked her. She had a warmth and nice personality that drew me to her. Over that time I never plucked up the courage to even try and kiss her and before I knew it closing time had arrived and they were playing the last song. She asked me if I wanted to go back with her and the group to their shared house. All I could think about was not wanting the evening to end, I wanted to carry on talking to her until the morning, I wanted to kiss her as well, but I couldn't do either. The fear of ending up somewhere strange in Leeds filled me with dread. I knew how to walk back to Andy's shared house from the city centre, but who knows where I would end up if I went with this girl. Who knows who lives at that shared house? What if I got there and she had a boyfriend she hadn't told me about, I could be murdered! Yet again, if I go with her, some magic might happen, we might even have sex, wouldn't that be great?

We all stood outside the nightclub, taxis filtering individuals and small groups away a few at a time. I just started to pluck up the courage to ask if it was still ok to go home with her when her friend started being sick in the street. Wonderful! Then all of a sudden it was a mad rush to get her friend into a taxi so they could all go back to their shared house. I stood there locked in thought as she gave me a peck on the cheek and in a flash, she was gone without me. I had missed my chance.

I spent an hour walking back to Andy's accommodation cursing myself for not joining them back at their place. I thought over and over about how many opportunities I had throughout the evening to go and I had thrown them all away. I tried my new philosophy, next to facing death, what is the fear level when faced with asking a girl out? Actually, of all the things that frightened me, that one thing is the closest fear to death itself. Women frighten the hell out of me!

As the year progressed, I grew in confidence. There was something about spring and summer that filled me with hope and positivity. The dark of winter always reminded me of how alone I was. In the winter it seemed like I just rotated from work to home and sleep and back again. As the days got longer, a feeling of possibility seemed to awaken in the greater daylight hours. I took the opportunity to go for walks as the countryside was on my doorstep. The fear of bumping into knuckle dragging violent locals, lessens somewhat when in the countryside. Even though open fields were just yards away, hardly any of the locals ventured there at all. It was a huge haven of safety.

-x-

My newfound sense of adventure had pushed me to spend a day in Nottingham a few weeks previously.

I travelled down with two intentions. One was to approach any goths in the city centre and pass on copies of my fanzine to them and ask them to send me a review. The other was to try and find a couple of shops that would sell it. Both were good ideas, but once again I was visiting a strange city on my own and I was full of fear and the panic that always goes with it. At least I was in the warm sunshine and would get home in daylight and not have to sleep out in the street.

I got a coach directly from near my house to Nottingham full of fear, hope and a bag full of fanzines. Walking around a city centre and trying to push myself to approach complete strangers was so very difficult. My head was screaming as soon as I got into the city to turn around and go home. I was full of so much negativity, telling myself how worthless and stupid my fanzine was and feeling tempted to give up and go home. It took so much strength to fight off a constant barrage of self-attack and doubt.

It wasn't going to kill me to talk to someone. This wasn't death, just communication.

I let myself get distracted and spent some time walking around trying to pluck up some courage. I walked around the city centre for an hour with copies of my fanzine in my hand until I spotted the most beautiful goth girl I had ever seen. She had the most amazingly beautiful hair all backcombed and spikey, had fantastically complicated eyeliner patterns drawn across her face and the most amazing eyes and smile. I threw myself into her path and approached with an outstretched fanzine. Her name was Liz and I asked her if she would take a copy of my fanzine, read it and then write to me on the address on the back and let me honestly know what she thought of it. The only way I could improve was if I knew what did and didn't work. Within a couple of fleeting moments and with the most beautiful of smiles, she happily accepted the challenge and carried on her walk across the city centre.

I had done it! Well at least once. I was so relieved that I had accomplished one task that I felt brave enough to have a go at my other goal. I looked around the city trying to find any shop that just might be interested in selling my fanzine. I found a shop called Void that was a proper alternative and goth clothing shop. It was an amazing place and I hoped so much that it would agree to sell my humble little fanzine.

I was so scared walking into that shop. The woman who worked there was very confident and that just made me even more nervous. I sheepishly started to talk to her, explaining that I wrote a goth fanzine and suggested that if I added a full-page advert for her shop, would she sell my fanzine for me. She could also keep all the money from selling it. My plan was to try and get folk to buy regularly and then negotiate a different set of terms later. I really didn't think I was selling it very well at all, but to my shock and surprise she accepted and said she would put them on display straight away!

She took ten fanzines from me and I made arrangements to go back again in a few weeks to stock up with the next issue and pick up the unsold ones. I came out of the shop on such a high and wanted to shout and punch the air in triumph. It meant so much to me to have a shop sell my humble magazine. I still had a lot of copies left in my bag. I had planned to give away loads of them to goths in the town and to do plenty of other shops, but I was so high and happy from having achieved at least one person in the street and one shop that all I could think of was how sad I would be if I went home after spending the rest of the day getting nowhere. I wanted to keep that euphoria and not ruin it by any rejection at all. So, I gave in and called it a day. I went home still in the daylight, before the evening came and before I would have to walk through the village in the early evening and run the terror gauntlet.

I was so happy with myself for a week or more, until I got a reply in the post from Liz, the girl I had met in the city centre and asked for feedback from my fanzine. It was so amazing that Liz had taken the time to write to me. I remembered that beautiful smile of hers so vividly. The letter was not what I expected though. I had asked her for honest feedback, because without it I couldn't improve. Liz gave me a whole raft of honest, blunt, blatant, in my face feedback. She was brutally honest, which was exactly what I had asked for. I was so totally devastated.

Liz highlighted the poor name of the fanzine, the poor presentation, the bad poetry and terrible artwork. There were a lot of things that I could include like what clubs were around and what gigs were coming up in different cities etc. There were a lot of things that I really did need to improve. In the space of just a couple of issues, I had become a lot better at making the presentation a little more professional. But there were also many things I knew I just couldn't do. I didn't know people that arranged gigs, so I had no word of who was playing where in the country. I also had no resources to get a computer and could not afford a printer as well. There were so many things that were out of my reach. Also, a lot of the poetry and art was reader contributed. I thought it was really sweet that people took the time and effort to send me contributions that I thought that it wasn't up to me to reject something that folk had taken time to send in.

The letter from Liz really knocked me down. I seriously thought about stopping the fanzine altogether. But I had to have a word with myself and pull myself together. I had asked for feedback and that was what I got. I was partially mad with myself. What did I really want? Blind admiration of a piddling little punk fanzine? I think I was getting a little fed up with not really finding my new tribe and even when I did connect with people, I still felt very different, very alien, like I had done all my life.

Then I got another blow. The place I worked at was doing quite well; there were a lot of new customers and some large orders coming in. New people were employed and a couple of us trained up the new starters. It was coming up to nearly two years since I started working there and after two years an employee got a whole load more employment rights including the right to redundancy payment when laid off. But as was typical of those circumstances across the country with the lowest paid labour force, before I got those rights, they terminated my employment.

I got a sense of deja vue. I had bought tickets to go and see the Sisters of Mercy at the NEC in Birmingham. So, for the second time in my life, I was going to see a band at a huge venue and I was going to lose my job at the same time. Losing my job, which was an awful job anyway, just made me realise how sick to the teeth I was feeling of working dead end jobs for little to no reward. Unlike the last time I lost my job, this time I had a different mindset. I was going to use it as a force to do something more with my life. I may have lost my job, but I hadn't lost my life. Losing my job was not going to kill me.

I decided to go to the Sisters of Mercy gig with my new adventurous and positive mindset. I was going to change the fanzine for the better. I was going to try and get into college. Losing my job was going to start a new chapter in my life!

# 7

## LATE SUMMER 1992, 21 YEARS OLD

I felt partly giddy and partly fearful. The fanzine had been going well over the past few months and I felt like I was reaching yet another milestone in my bucket list of achievements.

I was waiting for two people to knock at the door, so I was trying to be as quiet as possible so that I didn't miss them.

This was going to be the fourth band I had interviewed for my fanzine. It was going to be quite different this time. The band was local and were coming to the bedsit to see me for the interview instead of me travelling to a club. This was my first chance to try and fulfil the dream I had initially set myself which was to join a band. Perhaps if I got on well enough with them, there would be a remote chance that something may happen. They were called 13 Candles and were actually a goth band from my local town.

I heard a noise at the door and I went running to answer it. On opening it I was confronted by the most unusual pair of people. Louis, the singer and guitarist was tall and very thin. His clothes hung off him as though he couldn't fill them out. The other person was Justin and he played bass. He was a larger-than-life character, very full bodied, wearing a big white fluffy frilly shirt and he had big thick kissing lips. I couldn't help but think of Meatloaf when I first saw him standing there on my doorstep.

I invited them both in and led them through to my one main room. I made them a cup of tea and then set up my cassette player and got on with the interview. Louis was in his early thirties. He'd played in lots of new wave, rock and pub rock bands over the past ten years or more. Justin was about my age, early twenties. He had always been into thrash metal and had only recently become more interested in goth music through the link with Death Metal and that kind of music. I felt really mixed: whilst I was very excited to be in the presence of a local goth band, musicians that play goth music in this very narrow-minded town, on the other hand I could see so obviously that the punk element that really means so much to me and was a major factor in goth music, was desperately missing.

After the interview, I made a joke or two and dropped hints about joining them in the band if they ever needed someone. I asked them about where they go out as there was nothing in town at all that had anything remotely goth related. They told me about the goth nights down in Nottingham and asked if I wanted to join them sometime and go down in Louis's car.

I felt very mixed in my emotions. These weren't the people I expected, but they were still very nice and friendly. We agreed to meet up again and go for a drink and talk about perhaps me having a go at playing some keyboards with the band in a practice session, and also to go out with them to one of the goth nights at Nottingham.

They left with lots of promise and mutual gratitude and within moments I was on my own again, but excited at some possible future prospects. Could I have just witnessed the next step in my life, I wondered?

The following month turned out to be quite a rollercoaster. My life seemed to be moving so fast at that time that I feared it was spinning out of control. There was a mixed bag of ups and downs happening all at the same time. While I was very anxious about losing my job, I was also relieved. I felt free for a while.

-x-

When I decided that I was no longer going to church, that loss of routine was unsettling, but at the same time exciting. Being a Jehovah's Witness is purposefully formed to make you busy all the time. Church three times a week, each church session must be prepared in advance which can take hours, just like homework. Then there is going on the door to door preaching work and home studying. Throw in a full-time job, sleeping and meals and there is little time left for anything else. Then throw in the rule to not associate with anyone outside the church and you have a cult of total control. You can only see that once you are free.

Coming out of full-time work had a similar freedom. I wrapped so much of my life into something I cared nothing about. I was working hard to make someone else rich and to boost and stroke the ego of a couple of directors, for which there was no gain and a total loss of self-respect and dignity. You cannot have self-respect or dignity if you are always morally compromised or not allowed to be yourself or highlight illegality in the place you work. Work was so much like church, if your face fit, then you would prosper. If your personality clashed with an immoral, politically driven leader, then you were screwed. I didn't like to be in that position.

Initially I thought losing my job would mean going without food or having to move out of my tiny bedsit, but I found out that my wages were so poor, that I was quite a bit better off not working. It was such a shock to me that so many taxes and council bills and rent were taken care of by the state when unemployed, that the small amount of benefit money on top of that was much more than the small amount I usually had left over from my wages. That was such an eye opener about how poorly I was actually being paid. The fact that my employer could get rid of me just before I began my term of employee rights, just exposed the lack of any real moral responsibility. I didn't know why I was at all surprised. I think I was more disappointed that this happened while each day the smiley face from the director that greeted me was the same face that treated me this way. I still have such a low tolerance for hypocrisy.

-x-

The Sisters of Mercy gig at the NEC also happened a couple of weeks previously. I didn't want the losing of my job to ruin the day. I was really looking forward to going to see them play live. They were by far one of the biggest goth bands around at the time and although they weren't one of my favourite bands, the gig would be the goth event of the year. I had to at least be a part of it.

Once again, I was pushing my boundaries. I started with the most ambitious and optimistic opportunity. I sent the Sisters of Mercy a letter asking if I could interview them for my fanzine before the gig. There was nothing to lose by trying and even if there was only a remote chance of getting an interview it was worth the small amount of effort to try. There was no surprise that nothing came of that. The gig was also in Birmingham, yet another strange city to visit and face my fears with. Yet again I would likely miss the train home depending on when the gig ended. So it would mean another night spent alone, cold and frightened on the street which was not a great prospect, but it wouldn't be my first time anymore.

On the day, and in typical fashion, I took my rucksack filled with sandwiches, my camera and extra layers of clothes for the evening sleepover on the streets of Birmingham. It was a beautiful and red-hot sunny day. I wanted to get there early. It was an evening concert, but I wanted to arrive in the afternoon, just in case I got lost and I also hoped that there might be others like me that could be wandering around that might pal up with me if I had the courage to talk to them.

I got the train to Birmingham, arriving about midday. I hadn't realised that the NEC was quite a few miles outside the city centre and it took another train journey to get there. When I got to the NEC grounds, I was already worrying that there would be no chance of being lucky enough to catch two trains back home before the trains stopped running for the night. I was going to end up staying the night on the streets for sure. There was still a long walk from the dedicated train station across the grounds of the NEC to the actual concert venue. It was around 2pm when I was walking towards the venue itself. As I got closer there were little groups of goth kids hanging around and here and there were actually a few shy looking individuals just looking lost.

I ended up outside the venue sitting on the grass in the baking hot sunshine. It was such a lovely day and I was packed up with plenty of soft drinks and, of course, my sandwiches which I hungrily broke into. There was a lovely looking girl that was sitting near me and three or four other individuals on their own within a few yards of me. I plucked up the courage to start talking to the girl that was closest to me asking where she was from. I had hardly started up a conversation, when a young lad behind me asked everyone around him if they minded if we all sat together in a group so none of us would feel alone. It was quite forward and brave of the young lad and impressively everyone agreed. A group of about ten of us all picked a spot nearer to the entrance doors and sat together on the grass under the heat of the sun. As we all shuffled around and found ourselves in a circle, we introduced ourselves to each other. The girl I had originally started talking to ended up further away from me, which kind of stopped that discussion dead. Another girl sat beside me though and started to strike up a conversation with me.

Her name was Sarah. She was British but had lived abroad for most of her life and had only recently come back to Britain on her own to live. She wasn't very gothy looking at all, she looked more like a girl onto rock music really, but that didn't stop an interesting and long conversation happening about our lives. I told her about my fanzine, about recently losing my job and wanting to get into a band. She told me about some of her crazy life abroad and how she was now working in the countryside for lodgings and a bit of spare cash.

Sarah's whole life was in complete contrast to mine. She was very confident and very sure of herself. She had a life with no caution at all. Anything was game. She lived a life where she let fate decide her chances. She seemed interesting and very dangerous at the same time. I loved her confidence, but I struggled with her carefree attitude. I wondered how she hadn't been taken advantage of, used, abused, hurt or killed when she seemed to have so little in the way of a sense of danger. She gave me a few examples in her life where she had literally laughed at possible abuse and danger and got away unscathed.

By about 5pm it was still scorching hot in the sun and the group were struggling with the heat. Sarah didn't have a problem with it at all, she was used to foreign sunnier temperatures. The venue opened its outer doors and we all entered the building only to find that the inner doors to the auditorium were still closed and would be for a couple of hours more until about 7pm. So, we all kept our group together and sat down again in the foyer entranceway to the venue. The foyer was glass panelled, so it was actually even hotter than outside and we had hoped to get out of the sun for respite.

Sarah and I carried on our conversation for the next two hours and never ran out of anything to talk about. We were so different from each other. Sarah was daring and threw caution to the wind, lived a life of work and partying. I was a sad loner that loved music. Sarah loved music but couldn't get access to much where she lived. She occasionally went to goth clubs but had to travel a few hundred miles to do it, hitchhiking all the way there and back on her own. It was a different life and it made me feel privileged that I had lived such a sheltered life with such easy access to incredible and varied music.

We had been talking non-stop for about five hours when finally, the main venue doors started to open. I scrambled to find a pen and some paper in my rucksack, but typically they were about the only things I hadn't packed. I couldn't believe how stupid I was to forget something so obvious. As we all walked in there was a sudden panic that both Sarah and I got on so well and were about to be split up for good, so we hastened to try and formulate a plan to meet up after the concert later in the evening. But as soon as we got into the venue, being pushed along by the crowd, there was a sudden halt. The NEC had decided that they didn't like the look of thousands of goths. Some bright spark on the management team of the venue decided that anyone with spikes, metal belts, bracelets, chains and anything remotely weapon-like needed to hand in their decorations to a number of cloakrooms they had set up. They would exchange said goods for raffle tickets and could pick them up after the concert was finished. It was a gig by one of the biggest goth bands in the country, everyone was wearing spikes, metal belts, bracelets and chains. So, everyone had to line up and hand in half their clothing to a cloakroom attendant.

It took nearly an hour to get into the main venue. It was mayhem. Although Sarah didn't have anything to hand in, she queued with me and we continued our conversation for another hour. The rest of the group had disbanded and had all gone their own way to their reserved seats. Just Sarah and I were left together by the time I got to the cloakroom where I handed in all my gear, exchanging it for a raffle ticket.

Once again, we were about to split up. The venue was set up for about 15,000 fans and of course we had never met before and so had bought our tickets from the opposite sides of the country at completely different times. There was every likelihood that we would be sat at the opposite sides of the venue. So, we quickly agreed to meet up at the cloakroom after the concert.

As we both started to make our way into the main arena, we took out our tickets. To our astonishment we were both in the same stand. The chances of that were quite amazing. We made our way to the stand only to find that out of 15,000 seats Sarah was in the seat directly behind mine. It was so random and so absolutely impossible, neither of us could believe it. We were at the very back of the venue and although the rest of the seats were filling up, at the back there were a lot of empty seats. So

Sarah and I sat in some seats next to each other. If someone with the seat booked next to us turned up then we would have to move or negotiate a seat swap. But no one from the seats around us ever turned up. We both ended up sitting next to each other for the whole gig.

The gig was quite good. The Sisters of Mercy did like their dry ice and smoke machines. Nearly the whole gig was an experience of watching tiny figures way off in the distance playing on a huge stage covered in so much smoke that you could hardly see them at all.

When it was finished, I had to queue up again to pick up my bangles and belts etc from the cloakroom along with thousands of other people. I was concerned that we might miss the last train back to Birmingham city centre, so I told Sarah not to miss it and go and get the train back and not wait for me, but she wanted to wait with me in the line for the cloakroom, which was very sweet.

By the time we got to the train platform only one train was left before they stopped running for the night. We had managed to get there in time, but there were a lot of people and I wondered if we would fit on the train. The gig had finished earlier than I thought and I suspected that we might both get back to the Birmingham city centre train station before both our last trains for home left. It seemed possible that I might actually get back to my home town that evening instead of staying on the streets all night, although I didn't much fancy the last train back and a seven mile walk home in the middle of the night. I realised that Sarah might also get her last train back home soon. That meant that we had little time left together. I still didn't have a pen and anything to write on. I was hoping that I might have at least plucked up the courage to hold her hand or show some romantic interest before getting back to the station, but no matter how much I wanted to and no matter how quickly time was running out, I just couldn't push myself to take the risk and make a move.

All I could think about was how much my family would not approve of Sarah. How much the congregation wouldn't approve of Sarah. How much perhaps God wouldn't approve of me having a relationship with Sarah. She was too free, too adventurous, too unruly and without fear, caution or regret. I wasn't sure if I was fully prepared for a relationship with someone that different to me.

Sarah wasn't a bad person at all, I just wouldn't have said she was a good person either. She seemed to have no moral guidance, no thought for others and seemed completely free of duty to anyone else, which made her free of all those concerns. She was so different and refreshing to anyone else I cared to know.

I was still fighting internally with myself for the whole train journey back to the Birmingham city centre train station. When we got off the train, we were both in time to catch our connections. I didn't really care whether I caught mine or not, I just wanted to maximise the last moments that I could be with Sarah before she left. I offered to see her off at her train platform home, it meant that I would likely miss my train that was leaving around the same time, but I didn't care. By the time we had made our way to Sarah's platform, her last train home had already left. We had missed it. Because of that there was no time for me to get to my platform. Sarah and I would have to stay and sleep rough in the city centre and I wasn't going to let her do that on her own.

We found a quiet spot in the main train station around 11pm and huddled together on the cold marble floor. We only lasted about an hour before the train station fully closed down and we were turfed out. I found an outside market and from the wooden tables formed a makeshift shelter for the two of us and that was where we spent the night. I had enough spare clothes to keep us warm all night but none of them were needed as we never stopped making love until the morning.

In my brain, by the morning we were well and truly a 'couple.' With such an independent spirit as Sarah, I doubted that to her we were. We found somewhere to grab a takeaway breakfast and the sun again was so hot. It was such an amazingly beautiful day that we spent most of it in the city sitting around on grassy knolls not wanting to go home. By strange fortune we found some of our original group wandering around the city that day as well and we all sat together in the sunshine. Sarah and I were not the only couple to have formed and beyond my expectations, Sarah held my hand and let us lay around embracing each other all day. Eventually I found some paper and a pen. Sarah did not want to give me her address, but she took mine and she agreed she would write, then I saw her off at her train station later in the day. I took a leisurely trip home with a beaming smile on my face and got home still in the sunshine with no fear of the village at night.

-x-

Two weeks later my heart was still reeling from the high of meeting Sarah but saddened that she hadn't written. If I had her address I would have contacted her as soon as I got home, but I guessed that just wasn't her. I did think though that if she was remotely interested, she would have written within two weeks. Maybe it was over. I didn't have any belief in fate at all, but I was bemused how we ended up sitting next to each other from those prebooked seats. The odds of that happening were highly improbable. It did seem a shame if nothing was to become of our encounter.

I still planned to move forward. I decided that now I was without a job, I would see if I could get into college. I'd also had an invitation from Louis, the singer in that band I interviewed at my home, 13 Candles, to go to Rock City in Nottingham one night and to go to a Goth club. Also, I'd had a penfriend letter from a girl in Yorkshire who was part of The Cure fan club that I was also part of. Her name was Amshi and she wanted to meet up in Sheffield sometime. There was still plenty planned in my life.

# 8

## AUTUMN 1992, 21 YEARS OLD

I felt so compromised but I wanted it. I wondered where on earth Sarah had got that cannabis from as she didn't really know anyone around where I lived. This was the second time she had got me to try it. The first time nothing happened until I threw up. It was not a pleasant experience at all. Sarah put that down to it being the leaf itself and that I might be better trying the resin as that is a little milder. I didn't feel as sick the second time and I was starting to feel the effects of it in my head. I knew what my problem was though, it wasn't in my body, it was more so my conscience. Getting drunk recently had been a hurdle that I'd managed to get over but with many spills along the way.

I had spent twenty years being told how evil drink was. I was never brought up in a tee-total environment, but I was taught and had it drilled into me by the Jehovah's Witnesses that getting drunk was an evil sin. Whenever I would drink just a little bit too much to get tipsy, my conscience would kick in and an internal fight would start which would rip me apart and make me so ill.

I could feel that same conflict now. I realised with drink, that you have to let yourself get drunk, you have to give yourself permission. Nobody I knew had ever had to go through that experience. Once again, wherever I went or whoever I met, whatever I did, I was the alien.

I was trying to do the same with that joint. Stop fighting it. Let go of control and relax into it. It's a harmless bit of weed, it's not heroin. But it didn't matter what my logical brain said, my conscience ran mostly from my heart and it was my heart that still could not let go of the Jehovah's Witnesses' indoctrination.

-x-

I still felt attached to my indoctrination in a very negative way. I firmly believed that Armageddon was still coming and that because I wasn't a Jehovah's Witness anymore, I was going to die when it arrived. I was determined that I was going to be the most loving, gentle, kind and warm person that I could possibly be. When the time came and God was about to judge me and kill me for not being a Jehovah's Witness, I wanted to be able to stand up and say that I at least I was a good person. If God still decided to kill me, then I didn't want to live forever on a paradise earth with him as a ruler, I don't want that kind of God.

I looked around me and that mentality of wanting to be kind, loving, caring and a good person was so alien to everything around me. It was alien in the congregation because although everyone said that those are the qualities that they strived to have, their actions always fell short. Most Jehovah's Witnesses get so hung up on the minute details that they miss the obvious: to just love each other. In this outside world those traits almost made me a guru. I felt like a guru. Most folk thought I was weird because I was different. But if trying to love everyone made me different, than I needed to just hold my head up and be proud. Sarah thought I was a hopeless delusional romantic, which she wasn't always comfortable with.

-x-

No matter how many goths I met, I still could not find any of those dark romantics that I read about in Mick Mercer's Gothic Rock books a couple of years previously. It was so disappointing to realise that the beauty I felt in my heart could not be shared with anyone. I could share a moment of music with someone and that sometimes gave me a glimpse of that dark romantic connection, but it was very rare.

I registered at the town college. It was another part of my life plan as I'd hoped to meet more alternative and goth types there. I signed up for a two-year Graphic Design course. Even though the course was full-time, the college managed to enrol me part-time, so that the course could be fully funded by the government, and I wouldn't lose any of my benefits that paid for my rent and living expenses. The downside to that deal was that as a part-time student, I wasn't eligible for a student card, which meant I didn't get any discount on resources and transport.

I loved the course. I loved graphic design. It fitted me so well on two levels. I had a textural feel for artwork. Many times with my own art the subject matter was almost irrelevant, what I enjoyed was using different techniques to help the viewer feel the subject in a tactile way. I also questioned everything. So, when I did something, each element had a reason and when it came to graphic design as with every element of marketing, everything must have a reason in order to optimise its impact. For the first few months we mostly just concentrated on doing art, the same as an art class and I wondered why we weren't exploring more of the marketing usage of graphic design. I just wondered if that perhaps came later in the course.

One of the main reasons I wanted to go to college was because that was where I understood the core of alternative culture and different thinking would be. But once again I think I just missed the boat. For decades, universities and colleges were the bedrock of cultural revolution, where fashion, music and philosophy grew from, often encouraged by the tutors. But that was in previous decades. Now further education was big business and fighting the system was no longer the norm, in fact, it was very much frowned upon. There was practically no alternative scene at all out of thousands of kids, it was the biggest disappointment when starting college.

In the few months I was there, I did get some things out of it. The college had a printer and I pushed myself to go and talk to the staff that worked there. I told them about my fanzine and asked if they would print it for me, at a cost of course. The cost was the same as Ivan's photocopying, but the quality was much better. That meant I didn't need to trouble Ivan with it anymore and put him in a compromising situation.

I did one piece of project work for my course. We were given a brief and I built an eight-foot high black and white card poster of Jonny Slut from the goth band Specimen. He was adorned in a thick, huge black mohican, fishnets, ripped t-shirt, a feather boa was wrapped around him and he was covered in artistic black eyeliner with the words 'Gothic Punk' in large letters across the top. You could not miss it, even through the windows outside! I got a distinction for it and was so proud.

But sadly, I had to stop going to college. The cost of the bus fares every day and, worse than that, the cost of the equipment, was crippling. We were asked to do pencil drawings, oil paintings, charcoals etc, etc, and all that equipment I had to buy. When it came to a point where I had to decide whether to go into college or buy food, I had to make the wiser decision. Besides which, it was also at that point that I had something more important to achieve. College had to go.

Meeting up with Louis and Justin from 13 Candles had paid off. A major milestone in my life plan was going to be achieved. Both of them asked me to go to one of their practices and see if I would have a go at playing keyboards for them. We arranged an evening to see how we all got on and Louis, being the only person that drove a car, drove seven miles to pick me up, another seven miles to pick Justin up and then seven miles back to his house. Practice was to be twice a week and he did this for every session.

Louis lived in a humble terraced house and that was where we practiced. The neighbours must have hated him with the noise we were making. The band 13 Candles had only been together for a few weeks, but they churned out songs at an alarming rate. Louis had this awfully cheap little Yamaha keyboard that was only about a foot long. It had pre-programmed drum patterns on it which they used as a drum machine. It sounded awful. But they had so much enthusiasm. They would pick a naff drum pattern and just start playing to it and that would be it, yet another song. Louis would write down some lyrics or pick some out of a box that he had spent years accumulating. Or Justin had some lyrics that he would also bring along. I don't think either of them had any direction in their minds, they just played.

It was a bit of a fantasy killer. I had always had in mind great musicians with great minds connecting on an almost spiritual level producing a magical beauty. I had never thought of a random set of people banging out music hoping something wonderful would eventually come out. Don't get me wrong, both Louis and Justin were quite good players and did have a shared understanding that only needed a little bit of chat to get going. Usually, they started parodying a song or another band's style and then create something from that.

It was amazing in one way, the method of creating music, but in another way, it was so crude and accidental. I did see a lot of potential, but I also saw a lack of self-confidence and vision in the band. Everything seemed to be so amateur in its approach. The fact that I noticed something like that was really funny as I hadn't written a song in my life. Of course, I didn't say a thing. I was not a musician at all. I was a poor bass player at best. But I could see how goth music in the UK was very niche and therefore a goth band had an advantage of getting into clubs around the country with a ready-made audience. Neither Louis nor Justin had recognised that at all.

Already they had in the region of 40 songs. On that first practice they tried to get me to play the tiny keyboard along to a song that I had never heard before. While I was still trying to play to the first song, in their excitement they moved onto another song and then another! I came away from that first session with my head spinning and wondering what the hell had just happened.

It was like that for a couple of weeks, where I had no idea about the songs and hardly any of them were played through twice. There were so many songs and they were still creating loads more. I just couldn't keep up. Then on one session, just a couple of weeks in, there was a phone call to Louis which stopped the practice dead. The local pub in the town centre, the only one that played anything other than the trendy chart stuff, had a band pull out that evening and needed a band to go in straight away and play. Louis had been a part of the local music scene for so long and been in that many bands that everyone knew Louis and his ability to just go and play somewhere.

All of a sudden, after being in a band just for a couple of weeks, I was going to play my first gig. I didn't have a clue about the songs. Apart from 'playing' the keyboards, because the drum machine was on the tiny little keyboard, I was in charge of the drum patterns and fills etc. It was probably the best way to do my first gig, because in the space of two hours, I had gone from thinking I was doing another band practice to setting up gear in a pub and being thrown in at the deep end.

That first gig made me feel so sick. I wanted to throw up for the two hours before and all the way through the three quarters of an hour that we played. I was so frightened that I would bring the whole band crashing to a stop because I pressed the wrong button on the drum pattern. There were only a couple of songs that actually had any keyboards on to begin with, so that wasn't as bad as getting the drums wrong. I think I only got them wrong a couple of times.

-x-

After the Sisters of Mercy gig at Birmingham, I gave Sarah my mailing address and waited for a couple of weeks. Just as I was thinking that she wasn't going to write to me at all and that impossible coincidence of having tickets right next to each other was something to just forget about, I had a letter in the post. Sarah was not initially wanting a relationship but couldn't ignore how she felt. I was over the moon and walking on a cloud for a few weeks after that letter.

We wrote to each other by post for a few months and then she came to spend a week's holiday with me at the bedsit. That was a crazy week. We went for walks in the countryside, I introduced her to the band and then to Andy who I had made sure I kept in touch with. I took her into town to show her around the dullest place in the UK. We finished the week off by going to the Banshee in Manchester. That meant a train journey to another strange city and again with no prospect of staying anywhere overnight, as I didn't have the money and because it would be finishing late there would be no transport home. Sarah didn't seem to mind. The prospect of going to a well-known goth club was more exciting than the worry of where to stay for the night. Besides which, she planned to get chatting to someone and find a place to crash for the night. That seemed to me like a crazy idea, crazier than sleeping rough on the street, which I had done a few times by then.

We went to the Banshee and had a great evening. We chatted to a group of students that had a shared house and we all stayed at their place for the night. It was such a mad concept staying at a stranger's house and I found that perhaps not everyone that lets you go home with them is going to gang rape you or chop you up into a million pieces with their madman axe.

When it came time for Sarah to go back home after a week, we were departing to our different destinations from the train station at Manchester. I had an amazing week. Sarah was so different to me and she pushed my boundaries - boundaries that I still dragged behind me from being a Jehovah's Witness. One of the reasons that I loved being a goth was the way that it questioned taboos and stereotypes. Clothing gender was irrelevant, sexuality was irrelevant. It asked questions. What makes a person famous? Artistic integrity or fame for fame's sake? Because something is popular does that make it the best there is to offer? Why is marijuana illegal and alcohol legal? What is morally wrong with sex? Why does the Bible have a monopoly on morality? I was starting to work out for myself how a lot of Victorian Britain's attitudes were more about control than morality. But to push those boundaries was a very difficult thing to do with twenty years of indoctrination behind me. Sarah pushed those boundaries quite some way out. I loved her for it and I asked her if she wanted to move in with me sometime soon.

To my utter surprise that caused a huge shouting row in the middle of Manchester city centre. Sarah barraged me with a huge amount of attitude and anger that I just didn't understand. It became very apparent that the majority of that free spirit was a front, a fight, a rebellion against something deeper. I just didn't have the capacity to understand. I was going into a different place, where all that was needed in the world was love. Love conquers all and if I gave out enough love, I could change the world. I just wanted to find others like me, with a dark heart for getting to the meat of life and filling the earth with love.

We departed on bad terms and Sarah said that she didn't want to see me again.

For a couple of weeks, I kept on writing to her but got nothing back. I thought it was all over, that I had lost my one chance to have what Sam had said, which was to meet and fall in love with my very own 'goth girl.'

Sarah did write back after about three weeks, and she accepted my offer to move in with me, never telling me what had changed her mind and I didn't want to know in case it prompted a change of heart. She then gave everything up to live with me, her job and her place of residence were one and the same, so she left with everything she owned in the world in a couple of large travel bags. That is what is amazing about Sarah: that stuff doesn't matter and even where you live doesn't matter. The journey you are on and the people you meet is what is more important. Even though she was older than me and hadn't left a controlling religion, she had fewer friends than I did. In fact, for a lifetime lived, there was little to show for it, which I thought was a little strange.

# 9

## CHRISTMAS 1992, 22 YEARS OLD

I had hardly celebrated Christmas at all in my life. I had only had two with my dad's family and I really didn't get it. I understood that for small children it was probably an amazing day, but for me, it held no significance at all. In truth, I found Christmas to be full of promise with little delivery, typical of the western world I suppose.

Since leaving a controlling society where you cannot question anything, I now question absolutely everything, which I find healthy and refreshing. But not everyone wants to question things, especially standard traditions. I hear people moaning every year about Christmas, but everyone is afraid not to celebrate it. It's almost as perfect a controlling institution as the Jehovah's Witnesses are, where fear of being ostracised and not fitting in with everyone else is a primary weapon to make you spend money you cannot afford to spend. Scrooge is the ultimate 'devil' figure used to tarnish you with if you don't comply. I wanted nothing to do with it. Love is for the entire year, not just one day.

-x-

I couldn't promise Sarah a Christmas, so she spent a few weeks with some of her relatives in Scotland. In the meantime, I wanted to push the band I had just joined, called 13 Candles, onwards and give us the opportunity to break out from the small-town restrictions that most local bands get stuck in. I talked with the band about doing more in terms of promotion and thinking a lot bigger than the small town we were in. Louis wasn't sure of this energetic talentless upstart telling him how to promote a band as he had been in local bands for a decade or more. Justin, though, was a lot more open-minded with it all. I showed him how far afield my little fanzine was reaching and how many dedicated goth clubs there were around the country, all crying out for bands to play. The demand for goth bands outstripped the many numbers of goth clubs that existed.

My best friend Andy was now back home from university and had set himself up with his own business providing sound and lighting for amateur dramatic societies and schools. It was great that my friend was local again and it also meant that through his work he was now equipped with some nice new toys. One of them was a VHS video camera. It was quite the piece of kit. I talked to him about doing a music video for the band. So, between the two of us we worked out a plan that could work.

The biggest hurdle that we had, was that with an analogue video camera, there was a possibility that we could record small snapshots of video against portions of the music, but when it came to editing it all together, the sound would be jumping everywhere and out of sync. So, we needed a clever way of making sure the music played all the way through the video in one go and didn't lose synchronicity. We planned to split the video in two. One would be a single shot of the band playing against the music, with story line of interwoven shots breaking the main routine throughout the video. I had never done anything like that before, neither had Andy, but we were both willing to give it a go. The band were very excited but didn't have a clue about how to do it or to plan it all.

I started to write out a plan and then make it into a storyboard. The plan was to have Andy do the single main shoot around the band playing to the music track. Then we needed to plan out all the other shots and work out how to shoot them and in what order. It took quite a bit of arranging to get it all together. We split up the shooting into two days. The first day shooting was on Boxing Day. It was absolutely freezing. We all dressed up at home in the morning, did our hair and make-up at home before we then met up at the location which was a derelict hall in Sutton Scarsdale.

Sutton Scarsdale Hall is a ruined Georgian stately home located in a triangle of amazing stately homes on the border of Derbyshire and Nottinghamshire. Just a couple of miles away is the world-famous Hardwick Hall located just across the valley and on the other triangle point is Bolsover Castle built on the ruins of an older medieval castle. All three can be seen from one location. But Sutton Scarsdale Hall is unknown, even by most of the locals and access is open and easy. There is no entrance fee to pay, there is no access restriction, and you can walk all around the ruined building freely. It was perfect for shooting a video.

Boxing Day morning was clear and beautifully sunny, but that meant it was also very cold, just a couple of degrees above freezing. The grass in front of the hall was white over from frost, which straight away was a problem. Any footsteps on the grass melted the frost and showed a history of every step taken. If used, it could nicely frame both Justin and Louis on their spots in front of the hall. But if too many footprints were laid into the frost, it could divert the attention of the focus of the film.

The whole set up was very complicated. The video camera had to be held on Andy's shoulder as he roamed around the shot for the duration of the song. The camera was quite large and bulky. But the video tape recording facility was in a separate bit of hardware that could be carried in a special bag over a person's shoulder. The video camera and the tape recorder both had to be wired together.

Then at the same time, we had my portable music cassette player that played the song out loud for the band to hear and mime to. That also had to be wired into the video tape recorder, to record the sound directly with the video so everything would sync up properly.

Everything ran on batteries, so we were limited by the amount of charge on every unit. The cold also took a lot out of the batteries as well. The song was only five minutes long, but a run was likely to take about a half hour to set up, record and reset each time. So, time and efficiency were very important. I had to keep everyone focussed and sharp and ready to go in between all the technical setups and prep.

Louis and Justin were the main focus of the video in front of the camera. I was partly in shot and running around trying to organise everything, as a director does. The only other two bodies on set were Louis's and Justin's girlfriends. We used Louis's girlfriend, Jenny, to follow Andy around with the video tape recorder on her shoulder. All in all, there was the cassette player on the floor playing the song, about thirty feet of audio cables running to the video tape unit on Jenny's shoulder, then about another ten feet of cables running from the camera on Andy's shoulder to the video tape recorder. The cassette player was anchored to the floor and Jenny was anchored to Andy, so there was quite a bit of restriction that Andy had to work around while filming that one crucial shot.

We started with a dry practice run. Louis and Justin were freezing and getting bored. But everything looked great. The exception was me. I suddenly realised that we had chosen a track that had no keyboards and I still hadn't played on any recorded song by that time. The only thing I could do on the video was mime two little backing vocal spots on the two choruses, which wasn't even my voice on the song. The practice run gave Andy an idea of where to go during different parts of the song to capture different elements on film to match. Because I had done the storyboard as well, we knew which parts of the song Andy could use to move quickly around the set and have each shot ready when the inserts would be playing out.

After just one practice and knowing how cold it was, the life of the batteries and the concentration span of the band, Andy and I were happy to go with a take. It was going to be very difficult to get everything right and I expected that we could be spending all day in the freezing cold getting this difficult long single shot.

We got the first attempt underway. Louis just stepped up a level and really played to the camera, which surprised all of us. Justin was typically reliable and professional, stomping a green patch into the frosty grass. We got about two thirds through, and every little change and move was done exactly as we needed, Andy was in his element moving around in front of the Hall capturing everything as agreed but with a flair of improvisation that was also very much needed. Suddenly Andy had moved about as far as he could from the cassette player and needed to come back for the backing vocal part at the other end of the set in a short period of time. The sudden move back and across Jenny, caught her by surprise and the cables went to their furthest reach and the video tape recorder was ripped from her hands and smashed to the floor with a bang and a crash!

Everything stopped. Jenny was beside herself, apologising for dropping the unit. Andy said it was his fault for making the sudden move in the opposite direction away from her. We all rushed to the video tape unit. The case had come away and it initially looked like it was all over, and we only had two thirds of a song done, that's if the video tape survived at all and hadn't been mangled up.

Unbelievably, once the carcass of the machine was put back together, both the tape and the unit were ok and still working. Andy and I decided to get going again as quickly as possible before everything really did go wrong and our luck changed. Everything got reset and for the third time, we went for a take. This time it worked, and we got all the way through with only a couple of minor glitches. It was such a relief to get that done.

We then did some of the fill-in shots that were planned to be done at the Hall. One of the sequences was to pretend that we were all vampires, wiping away a bit of blood from our mouth after a quick human snack. It annoyed me how much goths were fixated with vampires. I got it, vampires lore touches a perfect mix of taboo, sexuality, darkness, beauty, androgyny and alure. But in the goth world it was like no other gothic literature existed, it was a little narrow-minded for me to fixate on one small part of the gothic culture. Still, it was a source of fun for me to add it into the video. The sequences were for the end of the finished video, where each band member wiped away the blood from his mouth as the camera swept around them. I did my shot first to show the other two how to do it. It should have been quick and simple, a small blob of tomato ketchup in the corner of the mouth wiped away with the back of the hand as the camera pans around.

I think it took two takes for me to do mine as I was smirking a little too much on the first shot. Then Louis tried to do his, but he hated tomato ketchup, it made him feel sick and he had a beard, so the ketchup kind of smudged. He still did it though, and then spat everywhere for ten minutes when the shot was finished. When it came to doing Justin's, he couldn't stop laughing. He kept messing around on every take and doing something silly. It took about ten shots to get it right and the shot we ended up with was him licking the tomato ketchup off the corner of his mouth with his tongue with a big dirty grin on his face. We were all getting a little tired so we let it stay in, and we just left it at that. A few days later we did the rest of the shoot in the grounds of a

Catholic church in the village where I used to live with my mum.

-x-

Churches were still difficult ground for me to walk around. As a Jehovah's Witness, churches were bad places to go and you only visited them for weddings or a funeral of an outsider, which was very rare as everyone I knew was a Jehovah's Witness. Even when going to a church for an outsider's event, we were told to limit that contact and get out of those buildings as soon as possible as they were harbingers of demons and the hub of the devil who dwelt in Christendom.

I love graveyards. They are always places of tranquillity and peace. Most people and kids have a fear of graveyards which means that for me they are a place to get away from people, especially late at night. On a lovely summers evening, they are a place to be peaceful and reflective, to honour and respect the lives that have gone before. There is also an element of facing one's fears. I was brought up believing in a spirit realm, so a fear of ghosts, demons and apparitions was very real. To face that fear and realise that graveyards are not a place to be scared of also adds a calmness to them.

-x-

All the remaining shots were in the graveyard of that church in the village. We filmed in the daytime and never went into the church itself which was closed, so I had no hang ups or fears at all doing the filming. Typically, because it was a really old graveyard, there was no-one around all day. Louis's girlfriend acted the part of 'the victim', she was doing an acting class at college in the town, which helped.

Once we had filmed two days of video footage, Andy and I used the video editing suite at the local secondary school to put it all together. Andy did quite a bit of work for the school setting up their stage and media equipment and also doing sound and lighting for their Christmas shows, so it was another useful contact that we were fortunate to have to be able to properly edit and splice the two lots of video together into a master tape. The finished product was incredible for a budget of absolutely nothing. The worse thing about the video really was the poor sound quality of the track. The song we used was called The Traveller. I didn't play a thing on it at all, as it had been recorded before I joined the band. It had that awful mini keyboard drum machine on it and the sound quality was really poor.

## 10

## SPRING 1993, 22 YEARS OLD

I was on such a creative and emotional high. Sarah moved into the bedsit full time, which was very small and cosy for the two of us. Neither of us were working and we both lived off government benefits. The living expenses for two people was less than two peoples benefit payments, so for the first time since leaving my mother's home, I had a small amount of spare cash and wasn't on the verge of hunger all the time.

A large alternative club at Nottingham called Rock City was putting on a special goth night with bands playing all evening. Five goth bands were playing, and I had contact with three of them. So, I arranged interviews with those three and hoped to get interviews with the other two by being cheeky and asking on them on the night, seeing as I would have backstage access.

Louis was going to take Sarah and I back home at the end of the night in his car, so Sarah and I took the bus down to Nottingham in the afternoon and met Trev outside of Rock City in the daytime. Trev was the guitarist for a group called Every New Dead Ghost and they were performing their last gig that night before splitting up. The band were very well known locally and had brought along with them a huge crowd of people for an after show party.

I took with me my trusty cassette player to record the interviews. Trev was a very energetic character that loved goth music and had a lot to say about the European culture, about where it had been and where it was going. He was the one doing most of the talking while the rest of the band got more and more drunk before they had even played the gig. Every New Dead Ghost were early to arrive at the club and were the first band in, a long time before the other bands arrived. Trev had a colleague (he had an Andy too) that was video recording their last day playing a gig and the whole interview was recorded, which just made me even more nervous. Sarah was a great help as she threw in some questions herself which helped my nerves immensely.

The next band to arrive at the club where Nosferatu. I didn't want to interview them again, but I did want to chat with them. They had just brought out their third record called 'Diva' on 12" single. I had brought with me their second single and the Diva single for them to sign for me. In the same way as when I met them at Sheffield, the guitarist was nowhere to be seen and never signed either of the records, just the singer and bass player signed them for me. They were both very excited about my copy of Diva as it was the limited edition in red vinyl. Even though it was released on their own record label, they still hadn't seen any of the red vinyl copies, so they took it from me, got it out of the sleeve and showed it around. It was quite odd to think that they had paid and had this record manufactured and distributed without them having seen a single copy of it for themselves.

The next band to arrive at Rock City was called 'Sins of The Flesh 2.' I knew the keyboard player. It was Tim Chandler who played keyboards for the first band I interviewed in Sheffield called 'Autumn of North.' It was great to see him again, he was such a nice lad and now we had something in common as we both played keyboards in a band. Sins of The Flesh 2 had about seven band members and Tim managed to herd them all into their one assigned tiny dressing room for me to interview them. It was pretty much the same as it had been when I interviewed Autumn of North; half of them were drunk already, there was lots of playing around and partying and I could hardly get anyone to answer a single question. The very short interview descended into complete chaos and Tim was so apologetic. All of a sudden there was a frantic scurrying outside the corridor which linked all the dressing rooms together. Something was happening.

The two remaining bands had arrived and were settling into their rooms and moving equipment onto the stage. The main headline band where called 'Rosetta Stone' and the other band where called 'Creaming Jesus.' Both where nationally established bands and were the two main acts for the night. The chaos in the corridor was because the members of Creaming Jesus had broken into the changing rooms of Rosetta Stone, stolen their guitars and hidden them somewhere. Creaming Jesus where a very rough bunch of working-class lads that played and partied hard, Rosetta Stone were a bunch of very middle-class pretty boys that took their mums to gigs. The boys from Rosetta Stone were never going to talk directly to the lads of Creaming Jesus with what troubled them, so as expected they went to the club's management demanding their instruments back.

It was all very childish, unruly, rock and roll and fun for the onlooker. I couldn't help but feel a little sorry for Rosetta Stone as I knew full well that I certainly wouldn't go against those scary looking lads from Creaming Jesus.

As I left the changing room of Tim Chandler and the Sins of The Flesh 2 crew, they shouted and warned me not to mention the word 'goth' to anyone from Creaming Jesus as I would likely be chased out the venue for it.

I had planned to ask them for an interview. Sarah

and I sheepishly walked past their changing room to the sound of smashing beer bottles, loud laughing and swearing and general boisterousness. As I passed the open door, beer splashed across the changing room and out the door nearly soaking me. I looked at Sarah and we agreed to give them a miss.

The only band left we hadn't approached was Rosetta Stone. They were in a bad mood after finally getting their guitars back. They had retreated into their dressing room, which was the biggest dressing room in the club, they were the headline act after all. At the end of the corridor the door was shut, they obviously didn't want to be disturbed. But I had a small fanzine, and an interview with them would likely make a big difference to the circulation of my little magazine. All the other bands were quite small and known to the goth community, but Rosetta Stone had been in national music papers and magazines, they were on the verge of breaking out into a bigger world. I didn't like their music that much. Once again in a genre of music that was born out of punk, Rosetta Stone were totally immersed in the world of mild inoffensive middle rock with a hint of psychedelia. Goth music was getting far from its roots and the genre was narrowing all the time in its vision. Rosetta Stone were yet another jingly jangly guitar rock band that happened to crimp their hair and wear eye makeup, so got tagged as goth.

I took a deep breath, knocked on the door and walked in. The main changing room at Rock City was ten times better than the other brick faced, stinking, sticky-floored changing rooms that everyone else was in. It was huge and had sofas and a beer fridge. The three band members of Rosetta Stone were very young, about my age. They were well dressed and they all had beautiful girlfriends with them. It was like stepping into the world of the beautiful people.

I nervously explained who I was and modestly asked them if I could do an interview with them. To my surprise they agreed. I put my cassette player on the table and sat on the floor in the middle of their group and fired away with questions. I asked them about what goth was to them, if they see themselves as a goth band, what they thought of the scene. I didn't have any questions written down. I had a few standard ones that I used, then depending on how they answered those, pushed them further for more. I asked the questions I wanted to know from the bands that I liked.

After about 20 minutes the interview was over and Porl, the lead singer, told me he was very impressed with the questions that I asked and how I did the interview without loads of written down questions in a fluid manner. He said he really enjoyed doing the interview.

I was on cloud nine when I left the room. I wanted to dance around the club I was on such a high. I had once again faced so many of my fears and just got on with doing what was needed. Sarah and I got a drink from the bar that had just opened and sat around in the main upstairs dancefloor area watching the sound checks continue ready for the evening show. I rewound the cassette tape to check out the quality of the interview recordings, I was so excited to have them on tape. You never know, in years to come they might be valuable bootlegs, I thought. But to my shock, the tape was blank. I wound the tape back further and nothing, further back and still nothing. All the interviews I had done for the last few hours had produced nothing! The microphone built into the cassette player must have been broken and had stopped recording. I was devastated.

I could have gone through all the bands again and redone all the interviews, but I was mentally exhausted, emotionally drained and finding the cassette blank was the biggest kick in the guts I could ever have received. I was so proud of myself for accomplishing everything I had set out to do no matter the personal embarrassment or risk of failure. And yet, without the proof on cassette tape, I could just be making it all up. I had a horrible sense that the fanzine would suffer because of this set back. I lost the motivation for the rest of the night. I started to take some photos when Sins of The Flesh 2 and Every New Dead Ghost played but stopped as the crowds came in and it became a bit harder to get close to the stage and get good pictures.

When I got home, I frantically tried to write down as much as I could remember from each of the interviews. The Every New Dead Ghost interview was still quite fresh and vivid in my mind, so with Sarah's help I scribbled down as much detail as I could remember. But all the other interviews were a blur. The one I really wanted to remember the most was the Rosetta Stone interview, but I was so nervous that I distinctly remember relying on the cassette tape so that I could use all my concentration making sure I had follow-on questions rather than worry too much about the details of the answers given to me. That left me empty without the recording.

-x-

One thing that did come out from the whole experience of the night at Rock City was that, despite all those bands, all those goths, all those fans as well that turned up to watch them play, I still felt so very different, still felt so alien, I still didn't fit in. I didn't particularly want to fit in, but I at least wanted some connection with a genre of aliens and creative misfits, which was what goth was about, a collection of creative individuals that all created in different ways. I didn't see that. Most people just fitted a pattern. It was an alternative pattern, but it was still a pattern of people following and mimicking each other.

-x-

In order to face my fears, in order to do something different for 13 Candles and to try and meet more goth fans, through the fanzine I set up a party at my tiny bedsit. It was in a building of flats and apartments. It was such a funny thing to do. My bedsit was tiny and in the middle of the countryside in a Derbyshire village. I didn't have a bed, Sarah and I slept on a mattress on the floor. So for the party the mattress was just lifted up and propped against the wall. You could barely fit 30 people in that tiny room, who knows what I was thinking when I set it all up.

My biggest motivation was trying to find a way of getting the 13 Candles video out into the world. To sell a video cassette with just one video on it I thought was a bit lean. So, I planned to do another video for another song, but also to do a couple of live performances as well. MTV was doing a series of acoustic sets by big bands of the time called 'Unplugged.' It quickly became a successful series and quite an original idea. Well known loud guitar bands would have their amps taken off them and ask to play an acoustic rendition of all their songs. Nirvana had done a very successful session and The Cure did a clever show as well. It showed how strong the songs were when all the noise was removed. In the same vein I arranged to do a short set with 13 Candles for the party and Andy would record it on video, then hopefully a couple of tracks could be used to bolster a compilation video cassette.

In the meantime, Sarah had some savings in cash when she moved in with me. Where she had previously worked there was nowhere to spend her wages and so she saved up a few hundred pounds. She offered to buy me a keyboard as she understood why I felt so embarrassed on stage standing behind a tiny keyboard only a foot wide with such poor sound quality and drums. Sarah took me into the town centre and we looked around the only musical equipment shop that was in town. The range of keyboards went from around £50 to over several thousand pounds. We needed to set a budget and just get the best we could for our money. Sarah let me spend £200 of her hard-earned savings on a keyboard for me to play in the band. It was such an amazing and wonderful gesture. The best I could get for the money was a Casio. It had 100 sounds and 100 drum patterns built in as well as midi ports, and the drums and keyboards volume could be controlled separately. It was so exciting to have a proper keyboard that I thought it was going to transform 13 Candles.

It was to be such an anti-climax. The drums were still very 'artificial', but at least they were a lot better than what we were using before. But then, the collection of 100 sounds and 100 drum patterns were a joke. Out of the 100 sounds, the vast majority were awful attempts at synthesising real classical instruments and sounded nothing like them or sounded so bad that they were unusable. It was the same with the drum patterns. Out of the 100, there were about 15 that were remotely useable. Try playing dark guitar riffs to a dixie beat with cowbells, it was just impossible. At least we had some that we could work with. It was, however, a vast improvement on the tiny Yamaha keyboard.

It was very difficult to avoid displaying a huge amount of disappointment in the new keyboard in front of Sarah, although with the budget, there was no way we could have done any better. I was very grateful and amazed at her generosity, it would have been very rude to have moaned constantly about it in front of her, so I tried very hard not to, not always successfully.

-x-

The band was starting to think a little bigger now. Justin got 13 Candles gigs in York through some family connections he had there. Louis got us an interview with one of the counties newspapers and it was obvious we needed some promotional materials creating. So, I arranged for us all to get dressed up and take my SLR camera out to a nearby national park called Clumber Park to do a photoshoot. Andy once again was the man to take the photos as I had to be in front of the camera. That session gave us some very good high quality photos to send out and use for promotion. A couple of the photos got used in that county newspaper article.

It was very strange seeing my face in a newspaper. I wore eyeliner, had a huge back-combed mane of jet-black hair and a full body of leather jacket and trousers and those lovely winkle picker boots I picked up from Leeds. A part of me was embarrassed. What if someone from the congregation saw that photo? It was very likely someone would. I didn't use my name in the band, I still called myself Black Angel as I was doing in the fanzine. But someone might have still recognised my face through the makeup. I hated the thought that I would give someone who used to be my friend and now wouldn't even talk to me in the street if they saw me, the satisfaction of them thinking I justified their shunning of me. I can imagine their attitude as it was an attitude I saw when I was a Jehovah's Witness.

"I bet he's a drunk, a drug taker and a fornicator!" they would say.

Unfortunately, they would have been right to think that way, I was all those things and knowing that made me feel ill so many times from guilt. I had twenty years of being told that someone with my current lifestyle was not just bad, but possessed and evil. The fact that I was a former Jehovah's Witness made me even worse than an evildoer. I was virtually unforgivable in God's eyes because I knew that what I was doing was bad, but I did it anyway.

I still feared Armageddon. I knew it is coming, and I thought I was going to die. I thought that any god that didn't know my heart wasn't a god. Any god that knew my heart but still felt the need to kill me to 'cleanse' his planet from those who are bad, I didn't want to worship anyway. That is where my heart was. This was the moral question that underlined my whole persona. Why does sexual morality matter if it doesn't hurt anyone? If I display unconditional love, then surely that is greater than any moral rule set by people with political motives and controlling desires and not those of love. I loved everyone, I wanted to fall in love with everyone. I wanted to give my intense love to anyone that wanted a share of it. I almost felt proud of that intensity of love. Why would a god not respect me for that?

So now 13 Candles had nearly enough videos to put a half hour video cassette together. We recorded a couple of live videos that were quite poor as they were very dark (in a nightclub? What a surprise). We had a couple of songs from the acoustic set from the party in my bedsit. Then we had the first video I directed called 'The Traveller' so we needed just one more video. Justin wrote an incredible song called Lost Child that I thought was quite amazing compared to the usual songs that 13 Candles created, so I suggested we use that song for another video. Justin was fearful that his girlfriend wouldn't be pleased using that song as it was about their child. She was one of those girlfriends that always felt as though she should have a say in everything the band did, very much like the character from the film Spinal Tap. So, before Justin asked his girlfriend, I had to storyboard the whole thing and I then talked to her directly and explained that the video would be done with as much sensitivity as I could muster.

The recording went quite well except for the base video we used as the one shot to sync from and to. I hoped that Louis would show the confidence he had shown in The Traveller video and attack the camera with confidence, but he was vulnerable, nervous and fiddled with his neck pendant for the whole track. We did two takes and on the second take he was getting worse. He also forgot the lyrics on one of the takes and was miming the wrong words, so we had to do a third take. But he was getting even worse and fiddling more with his necklace. So, I had to wrap it up and try and fill the video with as many fill-ins as possible. Andy and I were able to use the cuts with a bit more ad lib to cover up the pieces we didn't like rather than follow the storyboard to the intended design. I think the song was better, but the video was not as good. Thankfully, Justin's girlfriend still liked the video.

At the time it was quite unique for a small band to have a video released. Justin was the guy to promote that fact. He was really good at writing letters to fans and talking to fans on the phone around the country. He found a guy in Derbyshire that had a video exchange service and convinced him to include one of the 13 Candles videos whenever he put a compilation together for one of his customers.

I then asked Andy to help us record a decent quality cassette demo to send out to promoters around the country. Andy had a reel-to-reel tape recorder which could record at a reasonable quality. All the demos done so far were of really poor quality and, although the band had loads of songs on many demo cassette tapes, the quality just wasn't there. So, we put aside a weekend at Justin's house to record four songs. We split up into different rooms with headphones on and we all played live, mixed into the mixing desk and then onto the reel-to-reel tape recorder. It was such an exciting experience, and we were all buoyed up by it. It felt as though we were going places.

From that session we created a cassette tape and every single time we went to Rock City in Nottingham we took a tape with us and pestered the DJ to try and get us a gig there. After a few months of constantly requesting a gig, Rock City eventually agreed to put us on, probably to shut us up. It was amazing to play at Nottingham Rock City. I was so nervous knowing all the well-known bands that have gone through that renowned venue over the previous decade or so and we were playing at the same place.

# 11

## SUMMER 1993, 22 YEARS OLD

Our band, 13 Candles, played twice at Nottingham Rock City. Once supporting a local band called 'Die Laughing' who were a wonderful group of people and another time with Incubus Succubus who are also very supportive. I'd been developing my creativity and loving every moment of it. Justin liked to do flyers and posters for the band, but I didn't like his cut and paste technique from other people's photocopied artwork. His heart was always full of enthusiasm, but his finish was poor. He would just throw black and white pictures together and get a black pen and scrawl the band's name over it. He is a great bass player, but a naff graphic designer. So, I was constantly trying to create content for him to use instead of letting him resort to photographs from a book.

I created a backdrop for the band made from a thick white bedsheet and drew the band's name in coloured marker pens. It had a female vampire character on all fours. I wasn't so happy with it, it looked a bit Metal band sexist to be honest once I had finished it, but the band loved it and it got taken everywhere we played.

I was also getting more creative and daring with my appearance. I had made up my mind that I was going to die at Armageddon regardless of the way I dressed and since I came to the realisation that dress had nothing to do with morality at all, then I felt free and legitimate to explore my creativity.

The Jehovah's Witnesses religion taught me that any show of flesh was provocation, an invitation for unwanted sex. If a woman shows cleavage or wears a short skirt, she is asking to be raped. That is the mentality of the religion and I found it was also the mentality of a lot of men and large portions of society. The responsibility is not on the self to control one's urges, rather it's the fault of those believed to be temptresses that asked to be raped by the way they dress. It's when boundaries are pushed and questions are asked about what is normal and what is acceptable that such beliefs are exposed for exactly how disgusting they are. I felt almost a moral obligation to confront people with the stupidity of those beliefs.

I started to dress up in fishnet tights, ripped tights, a mini skirt, lots of belts and bangles, rings and silverware, clip on earrings, ripped up t-shirts. I wore ripped up tights over my torso and on my arms very much in the style of the Batcave club in London of the early eighties. It was great because a lot of people would ask me if I was gay or if I was a transvestite. It prompted discussion. I was always able to ask them why that mattered and how, apart from their own brainwashed expectations, they had come to those conclusions. I even got quite annoyed with some people because who I had sex with is a personal journey and no-one else business. It was funny how people think they have a right to ask because of the way I dress. I did have a lot of interesting conversations with people.

My penfriend from Sheffield, Amshi, wanted to meet up with me and Sarah and go to the Palais in Sheffield. That was the nightclub where I had interviewed Nosferatu months before. So much had changed since then, except that I still couldn't drive and still lived miles from any city and its regular transport links. Amshi offered to come all the way to Derbyshire and pick up Sarah and me and take us to the nightclub, which was such an unbelievably generous gesture and one that I took up.

The bedsit Sarah and I lived in was just too small. One of the ground floor flats became available for not much more money and we jumped at taking it. It seemed such a luxury to have a dedicated bedroom, a separate living room and a front door. That move meant that when Amshi came to pick us up, we could hear the door being knocked at.

But Sarah refused to go with us when Amshi

arrived. For some reason Sarah had decided that she didn't like this woman that she had never met and didn't want to go with us to Sheffield. I had to go. Amshi had travelled so far out of her way to pick us up and I didn't have a telephone to warn her not to come so it would have been extremely ungrateful not to have gone.

I felt a little uncomfortable at first getting in the car on my own and making excuses for Sarah not being with me. It must have been a little worrying for Amshi having a complete stranger climb into her car with just the two of us on a dark night. But she was wonderful, had so much energy and a great sense of humour. We didn't even go straight to Sheffield. We travelled 40 miles back to her hometown to pick up her boyfriend. Amshi's boyfriend lived with his grandparents. He was also a massive fan of The Cure and had met Amshi through the same penfriend letter writing invitation that I had met her through. He was already drunk when we picked him up from his grandparents. His name was Rik, and he was a very good-looking lad about the same age as me. We then went to Amshi's house where she lived with her parents. We all went into that house covered in make up and with weird hair, Rik drunk and giggling all the time and we had tea and biscuits and got fussed by Amshi's mum.

We then all got in the car and Amshi drove us to Sheffield to the Palais. It was so strange to be back at the Palais again and it seemed so different to the last time I was there. I was so different myself.

Amshi was such a socialite; she chatted to everyone, and Rik just got even more drunk and then started to moan like a big baby all night because Amshi wasn't giving him much attention. I ended up babysitting him most of the night because neither Rik or I knew anyone that was there. Amshi then drove me all the way home with Rik passed out in the passenger seat. She must have driven an extra 100 miles to take me with her, it was such a sweet thing to do. I confessed to her that Sarah had a problem with her, so we plotted a ruse for Amshi to visit one day and we would go out for a meal and Sarah would get on fine with her.

Just a few weeks later we sneakily managed to get Amshi and Sarah together and they got on like a house on fire and now they are the best of friends.

-x-

Many years ago, at school, Andy and I were in a computer club together. Although as a Jehovah's Witness I wasn't supposed to be involved with any activities outside of normal school time, for some reason my mum allowed me to join the computer club. Probably because there was only ever me and Andy that were in it and all we ever used to do was program the BBC micro-computers for games or just to learn the programming language. All my life I wanted to own a computer, but it was a pipe dream, impossible for someone like me because I would never have enough money to be able to afford one. Andy still had a BBC micro-computer and even now is still a whizz at programming it. He was so good that he worked out a way of making a Midi interface between his BBC computer and sending Midi signals to my music keyboard and play drum tracks. He made a little Midi interface box that plugged in one end to the BBC micro and into the music keyboard the other end. The clever lad then created a programme where the computer could play notes on the keyboard. When the keyboard was set to drum pattern mode, the BBC micro could be set up to play whatever drum patterns you could design. It was a feat of pure genius. Andy has always been a genius. That started to transform 13 Candles because we were not restricted to the drum patterns on the keyboard, we were free to design whatever patterns we wanted.

I had never owned a computer. They were always beyond my reach. Now they were desired because of the games you could play on them. A huge gaming industry was growing in massive leaps around this time and I still didn't own any type of computer or gaming machine. Sarah still had some money left over from her savings even after buying me a keyboard. She saw an Amiga computer being sold second hand in one of the local newspapers for £150. She offered to buy it for me. I was in turmoil about it. It was such an amazingly generous offer and made me question then why I wanted a computer and games machine. Did I want one enough to spend the hard-earned money of the person I love? I knew how other people think, but if someone offers to give you something, you don't think, you just take it. Sarah's money was worth twice anything I would save because it was hers and not mine. I would think twice about spending that amount of money on something I wanted, so I had to give it twice as much contemplation if I was spending Sarah's money.

We travelled and bought the Amiga computer for cash from a very large middle-class home some miles away. They were getting an Atari VST which had a built-in midi interface for a music keyboard, something the Amiga did not have and I found myself spending £150 and still being envious of something greater someone else had. I had to give myself an internal talking to about thinking like a spoiled child.

That Amiga computer was the greatest gift anyone had ever bought for me. Luckily one of my neighbours also had one as well and he had hundreds of games, so I borrowed them constantly. I felt for Sarah as the gift backfired in a way. I was so into the amazing games that I spent way too many hours stuck on the thing like a zombie not able to stop a game in mid-flight and just switching off everything else around me, including Sarah. Gaming is definitely a single man's hobby.

With my old bass guitar that I had bought as a teenager and my new music keyboard, I had enough equipment to make my own music. The keyboard had a built-in facility to record what you played for a few minutes, then play back that recording for you to play along to. That gave me two recording tracks in a manner. I found a clever way to record another track as well. With an old cassette player with the erase head removed, I could record both keyboard tracks live onto the left channel of the cassette player and then record my bass later onto the right track. That gave me three channels to play with. If I then looped that back through again with another cassette player, I could add vocals on, but by that point the quality was starting to suffer with tape hiss quite badly. Still, it meant that I could put together ideas for songs quite successfully.

I made a couple of attempts at doing songs and they sounded kind of okay, but there was something not quite right about them. I played one of them to Andy and he pointed out how chords and keys work in a song. Some notes fit naturally together in a chord, a collection of notes that complement each other. If a note is used that isn't part of the chord, it sounds out of key and doesn't harmonise with the rest of the song. At first, I didn't get it. I wanted to rip up the rule book, not conform to it. But in order to use disharmony properly, you need to know what harmony is in the first place. I learned very quickly to comply to these natural rules.

I tried to sing to one of my tracks, but I was so nervous about doing it. I didn't sing in public at all. I didn't dance in public until recently. I was so embarrassed. I was the audience I was most afraid of, the worse critic. At first, I tried to get Sarah to have a go at singing, but I just couldn't get her to do it. Even after several attempts at persuasion, she flatly refused to even try. That forced me into the position of having to have a go myself. It caused such an internal conflict. Once again, I knew that this was nothing. Singing out loud is not going to kill me, in fact it's not even going to hurt. I think that the biggest obstacle was perhaps what was at stake. If I couldn't find the courage to sing, or if I was really bad at it and sounded awful in front of myself, then this whole venture of creating music for myself would be very limiting. I piled a whole heap of pressure on myself to be able to sing.

That first time I attempted to sing, I had to wait until Sarah was not in the house and I was alone. It was the middle of the day and I shut all the curtains in the living room so nobody could see me if they tried. I was totally isolated. I wrote down some words and played the track around and around, singing so very quietly in the room with the music loud enough to drown out my voice from anyone outside possibly listening in. I was physically shaking with fear the whole time. The fact that I was so nervous in front of myself just made me feel even more pathetic which piled on the pressure I put on myself. Eventually, after lots of run throughs, I felt comfortable enough with what I was singing to have a go at recording it. I hated my voice, I hated it a lot. I have a tinny, whiny voice that's really grating and annoying.

-x-

Self-doubt is very much a part of my personality. I have always had to violently fight with my self-deprecation. I'm never good enough at anything despite how much effort I put in. I have seen the same trait in others, and it annoys me because it comes across to me as a whining attempt to get attention. So, I try and see myself in that third person, watching myself moaning about not being good enough and that I can't do anything and try and snap myself out of it.

-X-

I got really bad nerves every time I played live. Before a gig I felt very sick and wanted to vomit. As the time got nearer to going on stage, I started to shake and get dizzy. There was no part of me for some reason that thought that there was a way out of it. It didn't seem to be an option to not go on stage, after all this was what I always wanted. I think when I have made a promise or agreement to play, it would be immoral to not go through with it. I suppose the time to say no was when the gig was arranged, but I never protested, what would be the point? It was what I want to do really. Each gig we played, I arrived with butterflies in my stomach. Walking into the venue usually started the anxiety building. I then spent the time after the sound check hoping that the gig would get cancelled because I felt so sick with fear that I just wanted to die. Every time, the period straight after we finished playing was always the best bit. As I climbed off stage, that was when I wanted to turn around and go straight back on again.

That same fear kicked in when I tried to sing in front of just myself. I was anxious and embarrassed in front of no-one else but me. What I accomplished though far exceeded the pain, anxiety and fear. I was never satisfied with any of the songs I created, but a song was always the best I could manage at the time.

-x-

I think every artist has a sense of perfectionism, but there is always a compromise, there has to be, otherwise a song would never get finished. The compromise is understanding when you have devoted enough time to trying to get it right. A song will never be perfect, ever. But at some point, the development of it has to finish. As time, age and experience progresses, the level of development gets higher and it takes longer to finish a song. Those first couple of songs were very poor, very basic and the vocals were extremely weak. It took time to realise that just like playing on stage, the more effort and the more bombastic you are, the better the performance that comes out and strangely the more the nerves are combatted.

-x-

When I played the first couple of songs to Sarah, she was very encouraging. When I played them to the band, they were less than enthusiastic. When you play a song in front of an audience, it really changes the way you hear it. As soon as I played the songs to the band, I could hear all the awful things I had missed the first time and that helped form how I progressed on the next songs I created. The band were very good though. They collectively decided that together we should create a song that I should sing. I had written a song called 'Hate.' It was very basic and looking back, quite crude. Lyrically it was about domestic abuse and my disgust of it. Justin picked up my bass line very quickly and even added a little lick to it as well. Then Louis added a guitar line to play between each vocal part. It was so amazing to hear it being played by a band. Louis offered to let me sing it, but I couldn't. I could barely sing at home with the world shut out, there was no way I could sing in front of the band, and it was even less likely I could sing in front of an audience. So Louis sang the song and it became part of the 13 Candles set. Straight away it was no longer 'my' song, it just felt like another 13 Candles song that we played.

## 12

## EARLY AUTUMN 1993, 22 YEARS OLD

Sarah and I were getting on really well. We had such a strong bond. We spent all of our time together. It felt as though we had years' worth of a relationship in a short time because neither of us worked and so we lived next to each other nearly every single moment of the day. Sometimes Sarah would go out for a walk on her own. I struggled to understand why. I wanted to spend every breathing moment with her. I think she just needed a break occasionally, a concept that was so hard for me to understand. I had spent my life alone really and didn't like my own company. When I was on my own I couldn't stop thinking and the more I thought, the more depressed and anxious I got. Everywhere I went throughout my life I had felt mostly alien, alone and different. I had come to embrace it, but I didn't feel alone with Sarah. I wanted to spend as much time as I could with her. The only time that wasn't in my head and heart was when I played games on the Amiga. Then the whole world would disappear except for the virtual world I would be in. Sarah would take walks just to be with herself. She was a very independently minded person and enjoyed her own company.

I hadn't been on a holiday in years. Apart from the odd day trip to the seaside, usually with someone with a car, I never got to just get away from home for a week or so. One of our neighbours had a mother that lived in Exeter and occasionally he would hire a car and go to visit her for a week in the summer. We cheekily asked him that if we paid for some petrol could he drop us off in North Devon and then pick us up a week later on the way back. He generously agreed and Sarah and I found a telephone number for a campsite in North Devon. I still had an old tent from when I lived with my mum, so Sarah and I just decided to take the tent, make it up as we went along and just enjoy being away from everything for a week.

It was supposed to be a romantic getaway in the quiet countryside. But I ruined the holiday by doing something very selfish and stupid. This was the first time in years that I had been anywhere close to Cardiff. Cardiff and North Devon are split by the Bristol Channel, a very wide body of sea between the two coasts. I became obsessed in my head and heart with the knowledge that Katie, a girl who changed my life and who also left me in a whole heap of trouble with the congregation, was still likely living close to where we were staying.

I had told Sarah about the story of Katie and what had happened a few years before, how we fell in love, how I stayed at her parents' hotel for a week and how we had a passionate affair. I told her about how afterwards, Katie felt the need to confess her sins and how I was never allowed to get in touch with her ever again. I had heard through gossip that she had met someone else not long after and had moved on. Also how Katie hardly had a slap on the wrist from the Elders in her congregation whereas I had months of disciplinary procedures, shunning, and public humiliation in the congregation I belonged to. I always felt so hurt and so damaged by the whole experience. Even six years later my heart felt torn to pieces, mostly from the fact that Katie never got in touch again and just seemed to move on so easily. That trauma left a scar on my heart and I had felt betrayed for so many years. The burning question of 'why?' for all those years had tortured me.

I told Sarah how I felt and how much I wanted to get on a ferry across the channel, go to the hotel and find Katie and ask her. I knew in myself that to go would be a bad idea. It was the past. There was no scenario where any good would come from facing up to her and trying to get answers. I fought internally with myself because I knew it was a really shitty thing to do - to drag my current girlfriend to the house of an ex-girlfriend from years before. But it was typical of Sarah to be so flippant about the whole thing and to actually encourage me to face this demon if it haunted me so much.

I used that compassion from Sarah as the trigger to spend the day getting both of us on the ferry over to South Wales. For half the journey I felt sick because I knew that what I was doing was cruel and heartless. It was a horrible thing to do to Sarah. But the urge to confront Katie was overwhelming as well. I spent the second half of the journey realising what I was doing and wondering what I was likely to be confronted with when I got to the hotel.

The ferry journey took more than two hours. Then we had an hour's walk to the hotel. I was so nervous when I knocked on the front door that I felt sick.

Katie's dad answered the door. I told him who I was, and he had no idea and could not remember me at all. That shocked me as I did wonder if he might have punched me because I had brought shame to his daughter and family. He invited Sarah and I in for a drink and we sat at the bar. The hotel was empty, and we sat talking about how things were. Katie was married and had left home to live with her husband. She was still a Jehovah's Witness and quite devout by the sound of it, so her 'sin' had not made any dent in her life in the religion as it had with mine.

I left with absolutely no answers and possibly even more questions. I had dragged Sarah, in the middle of a holiday, for miles across an ocean and against all common sense and all moral direction, for nothing except the shame I felt. After a quick free drink at the hotel, we had to leave and dash across the city back to the last ferry which we only just caught. We hadn't had time for any food all day and then on the ferry journey back to North Devon the channel was very choppy. The swell was very high. I always preferred a higher swell because my eyes agreed with my stomach so that was ok. I always had a worse experience with slight movement on a boat. But Sarah was having a terrible time of it and spent nearly two hours either being sick over the side of the boat or trying not to be sicker. I felt so guilty. She wouldn't have been ill if we hadn't have gone on that trip. That was my punishment for being so selfish and heartless over what ended up being futile and fruitless.

That put a black mark on the whole holiday and there was a noticeable change at home afterwards. My life seemed to change once again as Sarah and I moved from being quite insular as a couple to being suddenly very social creatures. Ashmi was regularly picking us up from home in her car and taking us with her to clubs either in Sheffield or Nottingham. Every weekend we would be going one way or the other. I really loved it. I was really starting to come out of my shell by being in the band and travelling around with them and from constantly going out to clubs and meeting new people all the time. I loved getting to know people and finding out how they tick. I was starting to feel like perhaps I belonged, although the group of people were very diverse and different in some ways and yet, in other ways, all the same. There were people from all different backgrounds; working class, middle class. some were older and had been into the goth scene for over a decade and some were just getting into it. Some wouldn't class themselves as goth at all, but just mixed in those circles as their friends liked that music. There was a regular group of people that would be at both Sheffield and Nottingham and then there were some that were only at one or other of the cities.

I tried to make sure that if a new face turned up at a club, that I talked to them and got them introduced to the regulars. I was looking forward to each weekend and socialising with all the people I knew. The downside to that was the amount of drinking I was doing. I noticed a few unfortunate people that would get ridiculously drunk nearly every weekend. It got to a point where folk would steer clear of them as they were a nuisance and would just act drunk in a very sad and annoying way. You knew that they drank to escape from their life, but it never seemed to work as they were always over emotional and miserable. Because I was always there and I listened to people, I became a magnet for drunks wallowing in their drunken misery. I sympathised with them but struggled to talk or reason with them because when drunk they couldn't listen to me and make any sense of the world when they were in that state. So, I always tried and get to them before they had too much to drink and work with them to talk through their problems. I had definitely become a bit of an agony aunt, a person to go to when upset or when needing a shoulder to cry on. By the time someone was drunk again, it was pointless talking to them and it became annoying. I could see why other people steered clear of them and kept their distance.

The whole clubbing scene became a steep learning curve. Everyone was there to escape, to get away from the dreary life outside. But I had never understood escapism. Of course, I was raised to realise that drink, drugs and sex aren't an answer to solving one's problems. Most of the time people don't want advice and guidance, they just want someone to listen while they pour their heart out. I was getting to be quite good at that as well as giving out hugs.

I'm a very huggy person and I think that an embrace does a thousand times more than any words can do.

I also learned another strange quirk of nightclubs. Everyone says they are the best of friends and yet, outside of the nightclub, there is practically no contact at all. It's just like the Jehovah's Witnesses all over again. If someone doesn't go out for a couple of weeks, no-one checks up on them, no-one takes the time to make sure they are alright. Occasionally some people do act more like the friends I would expect them to be, but that's usually when they have known them outside the nightclub environment beforehand anyway.

The goth community could be very cliquey. There were always people who thought they were cool and that other people weren't. Regional cliques, cliques of EBM music fans, cliques of traditional goth, cliques of rock goths. They all struggled to intermingle. Both Ashmi and I were of the same opinion that cliques are just silly, and we went out of our way to try and bring the factions together.

I then learned another nightclub rule which I thought was just stupid, but many people had a problem with me for the choice I made. Ashmi had a new boyfriend and I was good friends with him, I really enjoyed his company. They had been seeing each other for about a month. We were at the nightclub in Sheffield and I saw him in full embrace mixing tongues with another girl openly in the nightclub. So, I asked him what he was doing while Ashmi's back was turned. He told me that they weren't getting on that well and it would be a blessing if Ashmi knew anyway, so he didn't care.

I cared. I didn't want Ashmi thinking she was in a good relationship to suddenly be confronted with that scene in public. I also knew that if Ashmi knew what I had seen and I had not said anything to her, she would rightly be very annoyed with me and feel betrayed. I knew what the right thing to do was. Ashmi had been my friend for longer, I thought I should tell her. I asked Sarah her opinion and she said I should say nothing and not get involved as it was none of my business. I couldn't believe Sarah said that about her very close friend. By saying nothing, I would be taking the other side and betraying Ashmi. I was so disappointed in Sarah for having that attitude. So, I told Ashmi.

Ashmi was very angry with me for telling her.

I couldn't believe the world I had dropped myself into, this society was just as awful and deceptive and political as the Jehovah's Witnesses were.

I learned so many lessons in such a short period of time, it was surprising that I wasn't put off clubbing altogether. But Sarah loved it and I did enjoy other aspects of it. Drinking every weekend meant that I was drinking more and more to the point that my tolerance was building. I thought it was cool to get drunk and play about. Then one day, one particular person gave me 'that' look and moved away from me. I had done exactly the same when someone was just annoyingly drunk and not remotely funny at all. The party for one I was having was not a party for anyone else. When I came to that realisation - that I was that annoying drunk that everyone tries to steer clear of - I stopped drinking, I was bored with it. In replacement I started to drink Coca Cola. The caffeine and sugar gave me an energy rush that sent me crazy, where I would dance and run around with so much energy that loads of people would ask me where I was getting my drugs from. I still have an occasional alcoholic drink, but mostly I drink Coke.

All this energy and newfound confidence as well

as Sarah's drive to be carefree and experimental made me fully experiment with my hair and clothes. I started to shave the sides of my head, a bit higher every few weeks until I had a mohican about three inches wide. I had it dyed jet black, crimped it and backcombed it, then covered it in hairspray every time I went out. Sarah then started doing the same with her hair. It could take anything up to three hours to get ready for a night out. Sarah and I did each other's hair because it was impossible to do my own as I couldn't see the back or top of my own head. The most shameful aspect of my character was the tantrums I had if I couldn't get my hair right. It was a fine balancing act with my hair. It was so tall when spiked up that it could easily lean or fall over and when it did that it went from looking very cool, to looking very silly. Sometimes after three hours of work, my hair just wouldn't behave and do what I asked, which was always followed by a pathetic childish tantrum. I was such a drama queen. Hairbrushes, crimpers, anything to hand would go flying. I'm very ashamed of it, it was pathetic.

I had no problems with any type of clothing either. I would quite casually dress from neck to toe in ripped up tights and fishnets and even a mini skirt and high heels. If clothes don't have gender, what did it matter? What did it even matter if I didn't care what my gender was? As a male I belonged to the section of society that on the vast majority is responsible for rape, murder, war, greed, torture, child abuse and a hundred horrible things. I hated belonging to that section of society and declared myself out of it as a gender. I was neutral.

I decided that I was going to close the fanzine. It had originally had a purpose, which was to get me into a band. I was now in a band so it was no longer needed. It had served its purpose and to be honest I'd lost the drive to carry on with it.

## 13

## 3RD SEPTEMBER 03:00 AM 1994, 23 YEARS OLD

## END OF THE FIRST DAY OF THE FIRST 'WHITBY GOTH WEEKEND' MUSIC FESTIVAL

It had been yet another year in my life of the craziest turmoil. A rollercoaster of happiness and hurt, popularity and pain. I didn't know who I was anymore, I'd lost all sense of self and direction. My heart was smashed into a thousand pieces. I was questioning who I was and how I came to be here.

I was trying to sleep after one of the weirdest days of my life, and that's' saying something. I was wide awake, but emotionally and intellectually exhausted. Typically my brain just wouldn't switch off and shut up. I had a thousand things running through my head even though I was completely worn out.

I was in the dark, in the back of a van, with Andy and Louis. It was cold in there. They were quite happily asleep. Louis was actually snoring. Although I was wrapped up in a sleeping bag and a duvet, I could still feel the cold striking through with a dampness typical of a coastal early morning air.

I'd been lying there for more than two hours and just couldn't switch off. My heart was sinking, I didn't want to go out there, I didn't know who I would bump into. But I had no choice. Maybe the midnight coast would inspire my thoughts, calm my heart, give me some space to breath emotionally, spiritually and mentally.

As quietly as I could I got up and out of the confines of the sleeping bag without waking the other two up. I felt cold to the bone. I gently opened the back doors and quietly and carefully climbed out. It was no colder outside the van than it was inside, in fact I would even say it felt a little warmer outside. It was as though the van held the cold like a refrigerator. I took great care to close the doors on the two heavy sleepers, put my spare shoes on and start to walk away.

We'd parked in a car park at the top of the hill on the north end of the town of Whitby. From the car park I could only see houses and hotels even though I was on the top of the hill. I needed somewhere a little more peaceful, but I didn't want to stray too far in case I felt too cold and changed my mind and wanted to try and sleep again. I needed some sleep. It had been a very long day and we had another very long day ahead of us.

-x-

This whole thing started when a very close friend of Sarah and I called Jo, decided it would be a great idea to put together a little goth festival. Jo had loads of penfriends and was part of the Sheffield and Nottingham crowd that had formed over the past year. It was a great idea of hers. There was nothing like it around. It would have to be small as any large goth bands absolutely refused to have any to do with the word 'gothic.' It was a very dirty word and one that any band if they had any sense, would steer well clear of. Being very proud to call ourselves goth, Sarah and I offered to help organise the event with her.

First of all Jo needed bands to play. So, I got details of some of the bands we had played with a few times from around the country and gave Jo their contacts. Of course, being at the very core of the organisation of the event, 13 Candles would automatically get a billing and I could make sure we were as far up the order as possible. Jo picked Whitby. I think it was more because it was a mixture of things that ticked boxes. Jo was close friends with the folk that ran the Dracula Experience in the harbour, so that would mean she had folk in situ that could help if a local contact was needed. Also, Whitby would be a little more tolerant, we hoped, of goths walking about the town with not much trouble.

Being a goth provoked some strange reactions in the general public. Many were scared of what they didn't understand and got protective or just steered clear. Some, however, used that fear as a trigger to start trouble. Or some caused trouble because they thought it was cool to fight the weirdo. It could get very tiresome, so if the threat could be minimised it would be very advantageous. Whitby is a seaside town half-way up the British eastern coastline. It had enough hotels, B&Bs and rainy-day attractions to cover daytime activities. Everything about Whitby was perfect as long as we could find the right venue to host it.

So, a few months ago, Jo drove Sarah and I up to Whitby where we spent the day finding the contacts we needed to get the festival set up. We imagined, with Jo's penfriends and with all the friends we had in Sheffield and Nottingham, that we had to cater for at most around 100 people.

When we travelled to Whitby that day, Sarah and I had a massive row on the drive up. As with most arguments, I can't remember what we were rowing about. By the time we got to Whitby, Jo had to tell us both to grow up, like a parent scolding her children. That was so embarrassing. That was where the scales were tipping in mine and Sarah's relationship and not in my favour. The whole year had been a gradual slide apart. Sarah and I had never really argued that much before. I didn't like arguing, it made me drift into that horrible dark place where my depression lay. The dread just caved in over the top of me whenever I got into an argument with someone I loved.

-x-

I was still working on the principle that things I do will not kill me, but one thing that might, would be losing Sarah. That was a fear as bad as facing death. I struggled to even contemplate that scenario as it was so dire and horrible.

I think one of the switches that clicked in Sarah's heart was the same fear, except her reaction was completely different. She resented that fear. For Sarah that dread of losing me was a chain around the neck of someone that would never be bound by any emotional constraints. She started to tell me often that she felt trapped and resented me for loving her. What do you say to that, what can you say? I could only tell her how much I loved her and how much I also feared losing her, but that created even more resentment and accusations of emotional blackmail.

Emotional blackmail were two words that I just couldn't get my head around. I had always been an open and honest person and I couldn't understand how loving someone could be so negative, that it could be used as a method of abuse. I was abusing Sarah because I would tell her that I loved her.

We were becoming so disconnected and disjointed. Once we started to regularly go nightclubbing and make loads of new friends,

Sarah's independence and free spirit started to soar. There was a problem that I was being left behind. I was getting to scenarios where either I didn't want to go or couldn't develop at the same pace as Sarah. Yet, in some ways I developed separately and in other ways away from Sarah as she wasn't interested in doing what I was doing. I wanted to involve Sarah in my music creation, but she just wasn't interested. I wanted her to have a go at singing with me on some of the songs I was creating, but Sarah did not want to do it. I was also developing a lot musically in my tastes. I had started to get to know and appreciate the more extreme goth music, such as Sex Gang Children, Virgin Prunes, Birthday Party, Diamanda Galas, Inca Babies, Uk Decay and Ausgang. A whole other world was opening up to me and it made me a little sick of the narrow-minded music of the gothic rock trinity of Sisters of Mercy, The Mission and Fields Of The Nephilim. They seemed to be on a constant loop at every goth club up and down the country. Considering that music brought Sarah and I together, she didn't seem to take much interest in it at all and certainly had little interest in sharing my journey with me. I even thought it might have been cool to have done a comic book together as I wanted to start writing fiction. Sarah read constantly, but that never even got off the ground.

Sarah's path was more in drinking, clubbing and drugs, while I had got bored with drinking. Sarah kept on dropping hints about trying out the locally preferred drugs. Most people around us including

Ashmi constantly took Amphetamine, and some were partial to dropping LSD. Sarah had taken those drugs many times before in her life, but I hadn't done anything other than smoke a bit of cannabis, which was too extreme for me on the drug scale. I couldn't help but be put off by drugs. I knew enough about them to know how dangerous they could be, not from a side effects point of view, but from an addiction viewpoint. I was so annoyed that I was addicted to cigarettes.

Starting smoking was the most stupid thing I had ever done in my life. I was controlled by this chemical substance that I had practically no control over, which was sold for no other reason than to make money out of me. That dependency annoyed the hell out of me. Knowing my addictive personality, I knew it was unwise to get messed up with anything else. Also, if Coca Cola sent me into a state of crazy mania, then I hated to think what Amphetamine would do to me and with my vivid imagination I dreaded where LSD would send me.

When I looked around me at the people I called my friends, they all seemed to live a life on various stages of student limbo. This whole alternative and goth crowd were a mix of those that drink and take drugs and get over it and move on and those that get stuck in it and never seem to grow out of it or away from it, some stuck in that limbo for decades. I valued a different kind of freedom, one not dictated by chemical dependency.

The other thing that put me off drugs, particularly Amphetamine, is the 'speed strop'. Those that took speed regularly, got to the point that without it, they cannot have any fun at all. There were so many people that spent an entire evening sulking and virtually crying into their beer because for some reason that weekend they couldn't do any speed. I saw it all the time and it was quite pathetic. I didn't cry into my orange juice if I couldn't get any Coke Cola! Of course, drugs were used in the same way as drink as a method of escape and drugs, as a long-term method of escape, is always going to end badly. I saw many casualties.

I had never told Sarah she couldn't do drugs. How could I? She was an independent spirit. She was a person in charge of her own life and destiny. But for some reason she thought that because I didn't approve of drugs, that meant she didn't have that freedom and I restricted her choices. For months I didn't know that she did speed with Ashmi. When I found out she was doing it, I never confronted her because it had nothing to do with me. I was disappointed in her, but it was typical of her personality. If I had told Sarah she couldn't do something, even if that was perceived, she was more likely to do it. I was more shocked that Sarah thought that for months she needed to keep it a secret from me, as though my approval mattered.

I found this world so difficult to work out.

There was also another aspect of our lives which

had become strange and unusual, and I felt was splitting us apart. In Nottingham, a couple of promoters had got together to start a set of nightclub events called 'Fetish Events.' I think initially it was run by a guy that ran a fetish fashion magazine and he wanted to promote a local event to invite traders to sell specialist clothing and sex equipment but there wouldn't be enough interested punters to fill up an entire nightclub to make it worth it. So, he combined forces with a local goth music promoter to pull in the goth crowd which would create enough interest to be able to afford a bigger venue with enough space to put in market stalls etc. The reason goths were included was because they would wear a lot of fetish clothing in the form of belts, spiky bracelets, whips, PVC and leather clothes. It was a connection very much from the punk era. The Sex Pistols were really a bunch of kids wearing clothes from Malcom McLaren's shop SEX. In fact, really the Sex Pistols were a manufactured boy band created to promote Malcolm McLaren's and Viviene Westwood's shop that sold clothes and sex equipment. That was the link between goth and fetishism. There was also a link with the goth tradition of breaking taboo. Bauhaus were very articulate in highlighting the Victorian obsession with hiding sexual exploits and sexual expression and identity thereby creating a twisted underground fetishism.

On an intellectual level I liked the fact that the Fetish Events highlighted the stupidity of sexual taboo. I think it also created a healthy place for gay people to be openly expressive. Fetish can also be a very powerful way for women to be openly dominant, something that seems so backwards in the modern age that women are still expected to be weaker and subordinate. But as with a lot of events that strike a chord of popularity, it exposed some uglier sides of our goth culture. While for some it was liberating, I felt as though I was watching through a bubble as so much of it was exploitative as well. I don't mean by those that willingly want to be dominated, no, I mean some people who were exploited into doing things that seemed so obvious to me they didn't really want to do, but in order to fit, to be accepted or just to go with the flow, did things they were not proud of.

-x-

I had mixed feelings about the events. The first event had a few clothing and performance shows. They were great fun and it became a night of jaw dropping amazement. There were two highlights for me on that first event. The first was when two or three beautiful and perfectly adorned women in neck to toe shiny PVC came in tall, proud and prominent in their stiletto heels and long dark hair into the club. All of them had four slaves each, very well built muscley fit men that whore PVC covers over their faces, dog collars and very small PVC pants. None of them were allowed to get up off the floor all night and licked the boots of their masters and drank out of dog bowls. They all sat very well behaved all night at their masters' feet. Those women were so powerful. The other highlight was the gay show at the end of the night. The men wore big strap-ons and simulated gay sex on the stage much to the amusement of the audience but not the owners of the club. They promptly panicked and pulled the plug, shutting it all down for being too lewd about 20 minutes before the club was closing anyway. Those things were great about the fetish nights. But as each event progressed the cheaper and sleazier I felt they got.

-x-

I loved facing up to taboo, I think we should all question why something is banned, why something is classed as rude and inappropriate. Sex is something that the vast majority of us will do. We all have the same bodies, so why we should be ashamed of them is power politics and is just silly. Once again though, I have always had a difference of opinion to many. I have the opinion that there are two types of sex, selfish and non-selfish. I think masturbation is selfish sex, a functional basic bodily requirement and a human right to perform. But it is selfish and for self-gratification and I consider it to be as functional as going to the toilet. Necessary, but hardly something you feel the need to do in front of others, but also nothing to be ashamed of either. We all do it.

In my opinion though, as soon as someone else gets involved sexually, the onus moves from satisfying self to satisfying another. It's a wonderful and beautiful arrangement where two people (or more) become totally involved with each other in whatever way they wish and it becomes magical and mystical, even spiritual, because selfishness is removed completely from the experience. That has always been what I have found to be fundamentally spiritual about when more than one person has a sexual experience with another.

The problem I had with these fetish nights is that they became more obsessed with self-satisfaction than spirituality. It was all about 'what I can get' rather than 'what I can do for you', which was too near to rape, exploitation and brutality for me. There will always be a fine balance, but most people didn't even know there was a balance to be made. The female orgasm was still mostly seen as a myth in the nineties, which is absolutely mind blowing that that was even a thing, no matter the norm.

Sarah was totally obsessed with it all. She loved those fetish nights and thought that I needed to get a life. There were some big differences opening between us.

-x-

I breathed in the night coastal sea air. I didn't feel remotely tired even though I'd had the longest of days. I started to walk downhill hoping to find some peace somewhere. I recalled in the daylight that there was a grassy hill that stuck out separately to the rest of the hillside, so I tried to find it. I got to the

East Terrace and I could see the Whitby WhaleBone Arch in front of me further down the road. To the right of me I could see the dark shadow of the hill that stuck out from Bram Stoker's Bench (named after the author of Dracula). As I walked down the hill, I heard a small group of goths making their way up the Khyber Pass Road from the harbour front. They didn't make much noise and I made sure to keep well out of their way. I couldn't face trying to be civilised to someone the way I felt at the time. I paused and let them continue on their way making sure they didn't see me. Once they'd gone I walked down past Bram Stoker's Bench and out to the end of the escarpment passing a line of benches until I got to the very end and then sat on the grass at the top of the steep slope which fell away from me on all sides.

I sat and stared at the derelict ruins of the Abbey lit up across the harbour on top of the hill across from me. A peace started to descend on me as I tried to settle the sickness in my stomach. I was just starting to settle a little when I noticed movement all over the hillside across the bay from me. All around the graveyard below the Abbey on the hill, there were little lights and torches moving around across the grass, some of them so bright that they flickered across the valley occasionally in my direction. I could faintly hear shouting and laughter as the wind occasionally fell into a favourable direction and picked up the noises and blew them to me from afar. I thought of the distance and the amount of noise they must be making for it to reach me.

I couldn't help but think that once again I think like the alien. We have all done something amazing here and created a successful goth festival event and on the first night of it a bunch of idiots was going to get the thing banned before it's even started. I was so disappointed at being a goth. This was not what I thought my romanticism was going to be. I concluded that it was just the same as every other genre of music or general following of people, it was just an excuse to get drunk, take drugs, have sex and escape. It doesn't mean anything romantic, or important, or moving. It was another excuse to party just with black clothes on.

I imagined the party that was happening around those lights on the hillside. Partying in a graveyard is not respecting the dead that lie beneath them, there is no respect for the lives and wisdom that those stones represent. My heart sank. I felt so ashamed to be part of that selfish crowd. I strongly suspected that Sarah and Ashmi were up there with them contributing to the disrespect.

-x-

I think back to that day when Jo, Sarah and I came here to set everything in motion. We parked up the car and Jo had a hotel owner that she had made arrangements to meet with, so we went there first. There was a lovely lady that loved the way we looked and really looked forward to taking guests in for the weekend and also gave us some other hotels that she had spoken to that also had an interest in taking bookings for the same weekend. Jo was very encouraged by that, and we moved onto looking for a pub to host the weekend's events. We needed to find a venue that wasn't right in the centre so as not provoke any trouble, but had at least had enough space to load up equipment and wasn't in the middle of any housing so it would be a noise nuisance to neighbours. We hadn't looked very far and saw a pub a nice distance away from the centre but close enough to still be non-residential. It was called The Elsinore and was the first pub to try.

Jo didn't want to talk to anyone as she said she had no idea what to ask for. So, I was promoted to chief diplomat. I asked at the bar for the pub manager and this man came forward who looked just as you would expect a landlord of an aging pub to look, tired and bedraggled. I told him what we wanted to do, about how many people we were expecting, about the PA system we were thinking of bringing in, the dates we were planning and the type of clientele we were bringing. To my surprise he seemed very much up for it and very excited at the prospect of hosting it. So, at the first attempt we hit the jackpot. After a trip around the Whitby sites, a chat with the owners of the Dracula Experience and a chat with the manager at the Tourist information building, we had fish and chips and went back home, very happy with the day's achievements. It all looked like we were going to have the first goth festival in the UK.

Jo had done so well to get everything together in that short space of time. She was close friends with a band called Manuscript and we decided to put them on the first night on their own. Then the plan was to have four bands play on the Saturday night. The bands were All Living Fear, a band we had played with a couple of times, Nightmoves a band from Sheffield that Louis was friends with, our band 13 Candles and Incubus Succubus a band we had supported a few times, once at Rock City and are a lovely bunch of people. The Friday night would be filled with introductions and a goth pub quiz which I would put together and host. I was host for the weekend as well.

## 14

## SOMEWHERE OUTSIDE OF TIME

Sarah eventually told me what I was dreading for a long time. She still loved me but couldn't be with me any longer as she felt trapped when with me. I really struggled to understand. I just didn't get it at all. If we both still loved each other then what else mattered? That was my viewpoint. The biggest trigger seemed to have been when Sarah and one of her friends went to visit a fortune teller. The fortune teller told Sarah that her future was not with me and that just put in the last nail.

It then took more than three months for Sarah to move out of our flat. She was moving to Nottingham, that she was sure of, but didn't know where. I was so confused and hurt. She told me clearly that we were over and yet she still lived with me, slept in my bed every night and we still had regular sex. I buried my head deeply in the sand and refused to accept that it was happening as all the outward signs made it seem as if everything was normal. All my friends told me that I should throw Sarah out of the flat if that was her choice, but I couldn't end our relationship and how could I put the woman I love out on the street anyway? Everyone said that she was taking advantage of me. I was so confused. I tried to change myself, I tried to act as someone she would want, someone else other than the person she no longer wanted to be with. But I was always battling between my moral code and what I knew Sarah wanted.

We got so far apart that I began to see her as someone that I really didn't like but still loved. On one of the fetish nights in Nottingham at a club called Gold, Ashmi had picked up Sarah and me and taken us to Nottingham in the car. On approach to the club, Sarah and Ashmi stumbled on a wallet on the pavement outside. They picked it up and looked through it and there was about £300 in it, a printed wage slip and bank cards and the owner's address inside. It was a Friday night, so we all knew that wallet was someone's hard earned wages. It really bothered my conscience and I told Sarah that we should hand it in to the security at the club or even better take it to a police station the next day. I knew they wouldn't be bothered enough to take it to the owner's address because that would take too much effort, but at least we could take it to the police. I was outvoted two to one and Sarah and Ashmi split the cash between them then dropped the wallet with the cards back on the pavement. I was absolutely appalled. Ashmi was a very hard worker herself and I knew that if she lost her purse, she would be eternally grateful if someone handed it in intact. I felt as though I didn't know these people at all.

Then one night close to when Sarah was a week or so away from leaving my flat, I had the weirdest evening. It was the three of us as usual. We were going to a club called the Cookie Club in the centre of Nottingham. In the car on the way down to Nottingham, Ashmi, driving like a crazy as usual because she had taken a dose of speed for the night, was gibbering on and on about this man she had taken a real fancy to. This was the night she was going to make a pass at him. His name was Mark, a good-looking guy I knew quite well. He was a lovely lad. We parked up and went to a pub first. Ashmi went straight for Mark and were getting on like a house on fire. We then all decided that we were going to the Cookie Club and would meet Mark there as well. As we walked across town, Ashmi was on cloud nine, floating with happiness, still under the influence of speed and slightly drunk from a few drinks at the pub.

We had been at the club for an hour or so. Ashmi had disappeared somewhere, but Sarah had been talking for some time with Mark. Then while constantly looking at me, Sarah dragged Mark onto the dancefloor and started dancing with him very erotically. The glances and evil grin Sarah kept throwing my way told me it was a purposeful attempt to try and provoke me. I was getting more and more angry to a point that I have never been so angry before in my life. Sarah was putting Mark's hands on her bottom, she kept grinding her pelvic bone into his leg while looking over her shoulder at me, then kept trying to kiss him. Poor Mark looked so uncomfortable but didn't resist. He looked awkward but interested.

I was livid. The blood was rushing to my head. I wanted to burst out in tears, I wanted to rip off Mark's head with my teeth and I wanted to just go and die somewhere. Louis and Justin were with me, and they heard me saying that I was going to kill him. I have never felt such an intense all-encompassing rage and urge to kill someone that much before. I couldn't stop watching and a veil of pure hatred took over all my thoughts and feelings. Louis and Justin grabbed hold of me and dragged me off to the other end of the tiny club and told me that I needed to cool off somewhere before I did something really stupid. So, I kept away, dying, knowing that I had got there with Ashmi and Sarah and I would somehow have to get back home as well.

I tried to calm down, so I locked myself in the toilet for a half hour. This was death. All that fear I had confronted over the last couple of years was because I knew none of it would kill me, but this fear I knew intimately well, this was death. I wanted so much to just stop this pathetic existence. I couldn't stand the pain any longer.

I decided to get out of the toilet and get a drink from the bar upstairs. At least I would be nowhere near Sarah's public humiliation sex show on the floor below. When I went up the stairs and across to the bar, I noticed a figure on the floor. It was Ashmi. She was out cold lying across the floor unconscious with her head propped up against the foot of the bar. I looked around me, everyone knew Ashmi, but no-one seemed to care that she was passed out and everyone was just stepping over her. She looked totally out of it. I wasn't even sure if she was breathing. I became so mad with Sarah. She hadn't just hurt me, but she had purposefully stolen the man that Ashmi had been going on about all night and in the most humiliating way.

I knew Ashmi had taken speed, that was obvious. I also knew that she'd had quite a bit to drink in the pub and getting a drink from the bar was the first thing she did when we got to the Cookie Club. That was not a great combination. So, I knelt down next to her on the cold floor and tried to talk to her and make sure she was alright and still breathing. I asked everyone that was walking past us if they knew how much she had drunk at the club, but no-one knew or cared. I was beside myself with worry. Ashmi was the centre of everyone's nightlife, I was appalled with their passive attitude, angry actually.

As I grabbed Ashmi's left hand I noticed that her right hand was outstretched towards the wall and she had something in her fist. I pulled her right arm over and opened her fist. She was holding a bottle of paracetamol. When I got the bottle from out of her fist, I realised it was empty. I tried to wake Ashmi from her sleep, shaking her and tapping her on the face trying to rouse her, but she was not responding at all. I jumped to my feet and shouted at everyone in the upstairs club and pleaded if anyone saw her take the tablets from the bottle. I had no idea how many she had taken.

Once again, no-one cared. I shouted at the girl behind the bar and she told me to get the doorman as he deals with incidents. I was sure I was in some weird parallel world where nobody seemed to care about anyone. This was everything I was told as a Jehovah's Witness that life outside the church was like, a world where no-one cared for anyone else. I was right in the middle of that world, a world of fake friendships, a world without any moral sense whatsoever, a world where all that matters is the self and the short-term fix of escapism.

I ran to the doorman and he, at last, took the situation seriously. He tried to revive her and couldn't, so he called an ambulance straight away. He then asked me what I suspected Ashmi had taken. I hesitated for a moment. If I told him that Ashmi had taken speed, she could be in trouble, but then what was the point of trouble if she was dead. So I told him everything I knew. Between the two of us we managed to carry Ashmi down to an emergency exit out of the back of the club. By this time Sarah had heard what was happening and had turned up with a tear in her eye.

The cold air in the back of the club had revived Ashmi and she was showing signs of life when the ambulance turned up with the police in tow. Apparently, all calls of that nature, when drugs are involved, the police have to be called. Ashmi was really, really mad with me. She asked that Sarah go to the hospital with her and as she was being taken away, Sarah kept telling Ashmi how sorry she was.

Ashmi stopped speaking to me and blamed me for getting the police involved. I just didn't get this world at all.

Sarah finally moved out of the flat just a couple of weeks before the festival. At least that gave me some peace and quiet to get the final preparations done for the Whitby Goth Weekend. I had left putting the quiz together until the last fortnight before. I also needed to put together a few mix tapes as well. There wasn't enough room in the van to take all the band gear, the PA and everything to Whitby as well as a DJ desk and loads of vinyl, so instead I decided to put some mix cassettes together to play in the background all weekend. That meant that hours and hours of cassette tapes needed to be recorded to cover the whole weekend. That took me nearly every single night for two weeks to finish them ready for the festival.

## 15

## 2ND SEPTEMBER 1994, 23 YEARS OLD

## START OF THE FIRST DAY OF THE FIRST 'WHITBY GOTH WEEKEND' MUSIC FESTIVAL

We had hired a big white van for the weekend as space was going to be at a premium. The PA system belonged to Andy. He had bought it from a friend of Louis's who we used to hire the same PA from. Louis's friend still stored it for Andy as Andy still hadn't got a place big enough to store it all himself. Louis drove and picked up Andy and me, then we went to pick up the PA system. Andy had loads of gear; microphones, boxes of wires, mixing desks, crude lighting equipment, a lighting desk, cassette player and of course sleeping bags, toiletries, clothes etc. By the time we had loaded up the PA system into the van there wasn't room for me and Andy. Louis drove, Justin and his new girlfriend sat in the front, which meant that Andy and

I had to work out another way to fit in the van. So, we packed everything up to the doors at the back and left just enough room for us to lie down at the top half of the van against the rear windows. That's where we stayed all the way to Whitby.

It felt a little like an adventure. The sun shone on the way there and it was quite a warm day. I was feeling very nervous and so very dark, down, and utterly miserable. I missed Sarah so much. Although I wanted to carry on what I had started with Jo and see this great festival get under way, at the same time I just wanted to curl up at home and just cry uncontrollably. My soul felt like it did when sat on the caravan floor with the row of nine pills stretched out before me just three years before. My life had changed so much and yet it felt as though I had gone full circle and ended up in the same place. It really felt like a waste of three years, and I deeply felt as though I should have seen my dance with death through to the end.

I didn't want the journey in the van to end, I didn't want to go to Whitby. I spent the whole journey wondering how I was going to be able to function. I was at the lowest place that I'd ever been in my life and everyone around me was expecting me to put on a smile, pretend and make everyone jolly and happy for an entire weekend. How on earth was I going to do that when all I want to do was die? Then to top off that dread and fear was the prospect of bumping into Sarah with some other man in tow and watching her rubbing my face in it at every opportunity.

-x-

I thought about all those people that work in the entertainment industry and I suddenly had a newfound respect for what they do. Despite how they feel, they have to put on a lying face, smile and pretend that they're the happiest person on the planet just to give other people kicks. That thought made me worry even more. I'm still so bad at lying. I've never been very good at it simply because I rarely do it.

I thought back over the day with the warm night coastal breeze hitting my face. I was astonished at how much all those people I knew, who I'd helped through their problems, who had pretended to be my close friends, didn't even notice, or didn't care, how insanely low and depressed I was. I found it remarkable that I'd had to face this twice.

I leave the Jehovah's Witnesses, I stop going to the Kingdom Hall and everyone in that congregation that called me friend, all those family members that said they cared, never bothered to even find out if I was dead or not. Here I am more than three years on and with another completely different set of friends, people who I have become very close to and who I have struck warm and caring friendships with and all of them don't have a single care to comfort me, or to talk to me, or to even offer a shoulder or a caring hug. Nothing.

I am alien.

You have to get to a place in life and wonder if it is everyone else or is it you? I have tried so very hard to be the most honest, caring, passionate, creative, loving, spiritual, moral and sharing person that I can possibly be and it has alienated me from everyone. I just don't connect with anyone in the whole world at all. Once again, I feel like the whole world is so very cold and far away.

-x-

When we got to Whitby, we parked up at the Elsinore at noon and started to unload the PA and work out where to put it in the pub. Andy and I got to work and were getting everything set up. Manuskript, the band playing Friday night, arrived around mid-afternoon full of stories of masses of people saying they were going to come to the festival. I was still very nervous that the whole thing was going to be a flop and I hoped at least that the little pub we had chosen would fill up.

It took quite a while to get the PA set up. The Elsinore, although used to having bands on, didn't have much in the way of power sockets with a big enough supply on the mains board for the amount of power we needed. Andy, as always, was a genius in getting these sorts of problems solved and managed to get the whole rig working. Jo turned up without Sarah, thankfully, and started to get welcome packs ready for anyone that turned up. By 4pm there was a slow and steady trickle of travellers that had found their way to the Elsinore and Jo was greeting them and giving them a guide to the weekend's activities and details of places to stay and phone numbers if they needed help, etc. She was so well organised and in her element.

Louis took the van and found a car park to leave it in overnight. Justin and his girlfriend had disappeared as soon as we got to the Elsinore and hadn't helped in any way setting up the PA or anything. They had booked a couple of nights at one of the bed and breakfast hotels, so they had a nice warm place to stay and they both spent the rest of the afternoon getting ready and drinking. I was able to leave Andy doing what Andy does best - getting Manuskript set up ready to play. I had nowhere to get ready at all, except the back of the van, or the gent's toilets in the Elsinore.

I cared a lot about what I looked like as I was the compare of a gothic festival, but I had nowhere to do my hair up, or do my makeup, so dressing up seemed a little pointless as well. I knew I would feel under dressed and not myself. I wished that I had taken the time to book a hotel like Justin had. I would have struggled to afford it though, the whole weekend was pushing my meagre budget to the limit. It was a good job that I only drank cola.

I needn't have worried about the attendance. By 7pm the place was filling up to the point that people were spilling into the road outside. We did the music quiz about 8pm and there were so many people that

Jo was struggling to hand out the paper and pens to everyone. The place was packed with a couple of hundred people, and they were all taking their beers outside and lining up and down the road drinking and chatting. At one point some trouble started, and the Police arrived, but a local had seen the incident and told the Police how it was the goths that were the victims of the disturbance, and they took away a loud drunken brawler and left us all in peace.

I purposefully made the music quiz very hard. They were all questions about goth music and like a lot of good pub quizzes, the winning score was around 60 percent. I think I managed to put on the fake smile and fake happy face very well and just got through it. I'd never had to do something so difficult in my life, pretending that everything was rosy and happy when I felt the hand of death on my shoulder.

I do have a little pride in myself that I followed through with it. After all, I had promised Jo that I would continue, although I doubt she had any real understanding of what I was going through, the same as all my other 'friends.' I only saw a brief glimpse of Sarah. I nodded to her, noticed she was with yet another guy. This one I didn't know, which helped greatly, and thankfully I didn't see her again that night.

When Manuskript had finished playing Jo had a word with me. The Police had talked with Jo about the amount of people congregating and drinking in the road outside the Elsinore. The landlord of another pub on the harbour front had sought Jo out and offered to take the Saturday night event at his pub which was twice as big as the Elsinore. Jo had sought out my advice and although we would be betraying a verbal contract agreement with the landlord of the Elsinore, there were just too many people arriving, and more were likely to arrive tomorrow. So, I had to break the news to the Elsinore landlord and Andy and I had to strip the whole PA down, transport it to the pub on the harbour front and rig it all back up again ready for Saturday night. We agreed that everyone would still meet at the Elsinore first the next day, before moving to the new pub to get the first band on. The Elsinore must have made so much money from that one night as everyone was drinking all night.

While Andy, Louis and I took the PA down to the other pub, Jo arranged for a midnight exodus up the 199 steps to the graveyard and Abbey for anyone that wanted to tag along. I was annoyed that just a few of us got left with doing all the lifting work while everyone else carried on with the party, but I also knew that a party in a graveyard was going to be disrespectful, and I wanted no part of that anyway.

It was 4am and still the lights and torches danced around the graveyard across the other side of the bay in the footings of the Abbey. I was so mixed with so many varying emotions. I was proud of the way I had dealt with such a difficult day and yet annoyed about who I was, because who I was made me so different. I felt proud to be a goth, to have a heart that is so warm and loving, deep and affectionate, beautiful and passionate, but saddened that no-one understood my heart. I was ashamed to be a goth as well, if those desecrating the graves of those buried on the hillside across from me were to be called goths.

-x-

I thought back to what I thought goth was when reading Mick Mercer's Gothic Rock book, reading all those heartfelt opinions of the fans themselves and how much I connected with them and wanted to meet those with a similar heart. But I hadn't found a single one. Goth just seemed to be the same as every other culture, every other religion and faith, every other belief system, every other following, just a bunch of people agreeing with one or two influential leaders.

-x-

Finally, I saw the line of lights start to follow each other back down the steps away from the graveyard. I realised that Jo, Ashmi and Sarah were likely to be in that line of lights and they probably would come this way, up the Khyber Pass and past where I was sitting. I didn't want any of them to see me shivering on the grassy escarpment with tears streaming down my face, even though I was all dressed in black on an unlit mound of dark earth. I was feeling tired, so I thought it was time I tried again to sleep ready for another big day tomorrow.

I didn't sleep very well. Andy, Louis and I spend the day walking around Whitby, then finished setting up the PA in the new pub on the harbour front. The bands started to arrive throughout the day and we went through the sound checks for them all. The new venue was still quite cosy even though it was twice the size inside, but we were trying to put on four bands in a very confined space. It made for a very hectic afternoon, but we got all the bands' sound checked and ready for the early evening start. It was at that lull that I bumped into Sarah face to face.

Sarah asked how I was and I told her that I was about to do a gig, but I hadn't done my hair or makeup and because of that I didn't want to dress up because one without the other would look even more odd than it already would. I think because I didn't get angry or that I didn't just lay a load of guilt or emotional pain on her, I think she sympathised with what I was saying. So, she offered to do my hair and make up for me if I went to her hotel where all her stuff was. I was reluctant initially. I didn't want to talk to her new boyfriend, whoever he was, I certainly didn't want to see the evidence of the previous night's debauchery and I didn't want to be the object of any humiliation she might have planned either. I was really struggling to trust her.

I followed her anyway to her hotel. I felt so weak and pathetic. Despite everything she had put me through, I was still willing to do anything, be anything, she wanted if it meant a chance of keeping her. I could see how useless that made me.

I sheepishly followed her to her hotel room. Sarah then spends the next hour crimping my hair, backcombing it and applying my eyeliner and lipstick while I explain how I'd lost all sense of self since she's been gone. I tried to explain to her how I didn't know who I was anymore. That I'd become so willing to trade in everything I was to become someone I didn't want to be just to try and satisfy her and win her back. I was ashamed of how weak that made me and I was in turmoil about who I wanted to be. I had no idea who I was. Jehovah's Witness, goth guru, Sarah's puppet or a thousand variations of each.

Sarah was so kind and just listened and then weirdly apologised to me for taking one lost person and changing me into another. I felt I understood what she meant and as we headed back to the pub, I felt uplifted enough to dress up in my miniskirt, high heels and fishnets and put the brave face back on for another night of entertainment.

I hardly noticed All Living Fear play. I would have missed Nightmoves playing if someone hadn't accidently and drunkenly tripped over one of the power supplies that drove the main amp. The whole place went silent for a while. A few swear words and violent accusations aside, Andy got everything back up and running in no time and the festivities resumed.

I was so wrapped up in my worries - making sure all the bands behaved themselves and got off stage and then got the next band replacing them, that I forgot to get worried about 13 Candles playing. The whole place was packed to the rafters and even though it was a bigger venue, the whole street outside was full of black-clad goths chatting, drinking and listening to the music. Jo had done well, the weekend was a great success and there was already talk of perhaps doing it again the following year. Hundreds of people had turned up against all expectation and apart from a couple of glitches, we had managed it really well.

Then 13 Candles played our set. We had got to the point in our setlists where right at the end I would sing the last two songs. Usually, I would spend the set crapping myself in the build-up to the last songs, but because I hadn't had a chance to worry because I was so busy, I didn't have that build-up of fear. I sang the song that I had originally written called 'Hate' and then I sang a new song that we had all contributed to that I loved to sing called 'Sick.'

When I used to sing live, I always used to go barefoot so I could keep my balance as I threw myself around the stage. It's so easy to trip over wires and microphone stands and gaffer tape, so I found being barefoot keeps me a little more stable. I preferred to throw all my effort into singing. I would try and channel all my nervous energy into the microphone as it combatted the nerves a lot more when you attack.

I came off the stage with such a buzzing high, full of Cola and sugar and a decent reaction from the crowd - something 13 Candles didn't get that much of really. Instead of being bothered about organising the next band, the equipment packing up or anything, I just went and sat down at a table and let others sort out the mess for a change. As the bands swapped over on stage and Incubus Succubus set up to play, all the punters in the venue had the chance to go to the bar and get a drink, or nipped to the loo or find their friends etc.

I was sitting alone on this large round table and within a few minutes about eight or nine girls all pounced on the chairs around the table and started talking to me and congratulating me on the gig. The band never got any attention at all, even less so from female punters, so to have just one talking to me was amazing, but nine? I knew about half of them already, but they were all interested in me. From the buzz of the Cola, the thrill of singing with the band and now a bunch of girls taking in an interest in me, I felt like a celebrity. It was the strangest end to a weekend I had ever had in my life.

After two hours of female attention around the circular table, the music was winding down and the main lights in the pub were switched on and people started to be turfed out of the pub. I came straight back to reality and I then went to get changed into my casual clothes to start breaking down the PA and loading it back into the van. Justin was staying with his girlfriend in Whitby for a little longer and Louis was driving Andy and me back home straight away. It was such a contrast between the high of coming off stage, to the reality of packing the van and driving back home at two in the morning. Of course, just to make sure the mood was properly grounding, it started to rain, so no-one wanted to stand outside the venue saying goodbye or extending the chit chat. Within moments we were back on the road driving home, everything finished. Andy was angry at the roadies from a couple of the bands, Louis was annoyed that he had lost loads of money on the weekend as the pay he got hardly covered anything and I was lost and wondering where my life was going. It was a very dreary and dull drive home.

# 16

## SUMMER 1996,
## 25 YEARS OLD

Lying like a drunk on a cold, urine soaked, public toilet floor was no way to be spending a Saturday afternoon. My head was wet through from nervous sweat, my temperature was running high, I felt as though I was about to die. I leaned my temple against the side of the white porcelain toilet bowl to try and cool the heat pouring from my entire body. I felt so sick. My throat went into spasms and convulsions and tried to trigger my whole body to join in and throw up the lunch I was eating just a few moments ago. I fought so hard to stop myself from bringing up the cheap fried dinner that the struggle just added to the nausea.

My body shook and my stomach heaved. My mouth filled with water and sour acid. I was trying so very hard to stop my body from defying my will. I hated vomiting. It was painful and horrible. It was usually brief and I knew it was my body's way of dealing with a variety of problems. Throwing up generally is the start of feeling better, the process of getting the bad out and starting to recover. But I wouldn't let my body do that. I was different. My whole life had been different and because of that I refused to let myself be sick, so I fought it and the fighting just made everything worse.

There was so much going around in my head. The swirl and rush of thoughts, memories, situations and problems that added an extra dimension to my sinking physical state. Both mind and body were joined in their revulsion and conflict. There was a welling up of self-annoyance, pathetic pity, confusion and internal frustration. All that conflict in my head just fed the sickness in the pit of my stomach.

I felt as if I had the hand of death on my shoulder. The fear of that spectre surrounded me. I always knew I wouldn't live past thirty years old. I was obsessed with being a part of the 27 club, artists filled with a self-destruction that would implode at an early age, cut too short in life and usually in some awful setting.

This was a rock n roll setting ok.

It was just moments before that I was sitting in a cheap diner in the centre of town with my girlfriend and two of my friends eating a greasy lunch. We had waited 15 minutes for the food to arrive and sitting under the fluorescent tube lighting had started to put me under a trance. I'd had it before, that strange feeling. Although I couldn't see the flicker of the light above me, I felt as though I was retreating from my own eyes and into the depths of my own skull, a very strange sensation. I could see everyone around me, but it felt more like watching a scene rather than being part of it. The problem was when that started the situation just spiralled until I couldn't control the fever and sickness.

-x-

This new fear of panic is all consuming. Whenever I feel watched and exposed, I go into an overdrive of self-analysis. I split off from myself and observe from the side-lines and decide if I like what I see. I see a young man who looks very different to everyone else around him, a look that most of the society around him would not approve of. I can feel that judgement as one of those observers. "I bet he's a drunk, a thief, a drug taker. I bet he beats up old ladies and steals their handbags to feed his habit."

I dress differently, so that makes me an automatic failure. If I look ill, I must be taking drugs. If I'm throwing up in a public toilet, I must be a waste of taxpayers' money and should be left to die in the street. That is the general attitude towards someone who looks different. That then puts on an added pressure when anxiety hits me. I refuse to give the general public the opportunity to re-enforce their prejudicial stereotypes. It really annoys me to give away that satisfaction. That just keeps me stuck in a loop. I hate to give people their stereotype, so I don't want to be ill in public. That fear of being ill in public, makes me anxious and the anxiety makes me feel ill.

It's laughable really. Why should I care what people think? Why do I feel the need to be the one person in the world that can help change the way the world thinks? Why on earth do I keep thinking I'm right when the entire world is wrong? Does that make me some sort of narcissist, or am I what I think I am, a free thinking spiritually rich, love guru?

I'm a bag of nerves all the time lately. I think the strangest thing about depression seems to be that at the point that you really shouldn't be able to cope, you do. Then when your life becomes bearable and settled, the poison of previous depressions starts to seep out as though the body knows that the release can now be coped with. It has caught me unaware. I have the best life I have ever had, the most stable by far. My new girlfriend, Helen, is the most wonderful person I have ever met. Helen is a beautiful young woman, mild but not shy, humble and yet confident. She gets me, understands me and appreciates me. I adore her. Our lives are not rich, they are simple. But I have stability probably for the first time in my life.

-x-

After the Goth weekend at Whitby, I never saw Jo ever again. Our band, 13 Candles, returned to gigging around the country. We even played at the famous Marquee club in London once before it closed for good. I got more and more comfortable with writing music and singing. I was trying to gently persuade the band to explore more of the goth punk roots, but I was fighting a losing battle with them as their passion for Metalica and now Paradise Lost pushed them more towards heavy rock.

Every time I sang at a gig, I got punters telling me that I should start up my own band or sing all the songs for 13 Candles. That was happening a lot. A promoter in Nottingham took 13 Candles into a professional studio for a weekend. We recorded three tracks which I played on that got used on some European compilation CDs. He repeatedly told me that I needed to either ditch Louis out of the band or start a band up myself and he would be extremely supportive if I set up by myself.

I did think that Louis was a weak frontman. He was always so nervous, he hid behind his guitar, he was awkward, and he was always forgetting the lyrics or losing where he was in the song, which was difficult when playing to a strict patterned backing drum track.

But he was the founder of the band with Justin. Even Justin talked with me about finding a way of getting Louis to back down from the microphone and letting me take over. But for me, that was so morally wrong. If I wanted to do something different, I would be best controlling it all myself.

I moved out of the flat that Sarah and I had shared and moved into the town centre into a shared house. I had a bass guitar, I had my Amiga computer, and I had my keyboard. I had more than enough to create some music for myself. I just needed a name for the band.

My friend that distributed the 13 Candles videos around the country for us, knew of the terrible time I had after losing Sarah and struggling to find myself again and who I was and wanted to be. He suggested the name 'Personality Crisis' after the song by the New York Dolls. It was a perfect name. It described exactly where I was, where my music was coming from and the insecurity I had of where my music wanted to be.

I shuffled my arse on the cold wet stinking toilet cubicle floor. My whole body had pins and needles. I thought about my girlfriend and the two friends in the café that I had left behind. I bet they were wondering where I was and have frantically started looking for me. I just felt so sick and the last thing I wanted to do was projectile vomit in a public, crowded eating space. That just fed back into my anxiety and made the sickness worse. So, I excused myself quickly and ran outside. Once outside on my own I still had that same fear of what I must have looked like, pale, sweating, breathing heavy, looking like a street junkie. The only place of solitude I could think of was the public toilets under the subway in the front of the Theatre Royal. So, I practically ran there, found an empty cubicle and passed out on the floor with the door shut behind me.

No-one knew I was in there.

I wondered how many times that cubicle had been used to shoot up drugs, a sight that apart from the needle wouldn't look much different now. I try to get up, but as soon as I lifted my head above my body, the desire to vomit erupted again. I had no way to tell anyone where I was. I was completely isolated, which was the point I suppose. I tried to calm myself, tried and relax, let my body take back control from my head.

-x-

I loved writing music. I had a very basic programme on the Amiga that played about six tracks of 8-bit sampled keyboard sounds. It was a very difficult and long-winded process where the page scrolled downwards and I had to manually change the note on each line when and where I wanted it played. It was tedious, but it did give me some control over what I wanted. The 8-bit sound samples where awful and dirty, so I distorted them as much as possible to use them in a way that lessened the impact of such poor samples.

While I was writing those songs, I went to a party

in Nottingham at the home of one of the Nottingham goth crowd. He had started a band called 'Suspiria' with a friend of his. He took me around his house and showed me the makeshift studio he had created in a spare room of his city centre four story town terrace. He had a brand new Korg M1 keyboard that he was boasting cost him £1500. All I could think about was what I could do with that machine and the equipment he had lined up in that studio. All of it was so far removed from anything I could afford. Ok, I didn't work, but I was always worse off financially whenever I worked. He was so smug and full of himself. He had his pretty wife that got drunk at every available opportunity, wasn't allowed to have an opinion and had strict instructions to sit around looking goth pretty all the time. He was such a middle-class cocky dickhead it was unbelievable. Yet, that was what worked. He knew the right people and although the music Suspiria created was mediocre at best, his money and connections worked so much more than any deep need to create music.

I channelled all my anger, frustrations, loss, hurt, pain and confusion into my music and created two demo cassette tapes with Andy producing and doing the recording on his reel-to-reel tape machine. He also cleverly recorded the Amiga tracks, drums and some sound fills into another take to use as a backing tape when playing live, so I didn't have to use the Amiga as it was very temperamental.

I did call the band Personality Crisis and I changed my name too. I dropped the Black Angel moniker as it didn't seem appropriate anymore, it was also a little crude. Instead, a nickname for me was doing the rounds started up by a friend in the scene called Kingsley. I had got fed up with the number of copycats that were seeming to copy my dress and hairstyle in Nottingham. I saw it a few times. I used to change the colour a lot to try and see if I was being copied and to my annoyance, I still had copycats that copied the colour. So, to completely throw them off, I dyed my hair bright red and shaved half my mohican completely off, so from the front it looked like I only had half a head of hair. No-one was going to copy that! The nickname I picked up was Jonny Halfhead and even though the name was an attempt at ridicule, I really liked it. It conjured up punks like Jonny Thunders, Jonny Rotten and Jonny Slut. So, I adopted the name completely.

Everything around Nottingham started falling apart for me. It hurt so much to see Sarah out in Nottingham every time I went out clubbing. Ashmi wasn't talking to me anymore, so I didn't have the simple luxury of car transport to the city. Every time I went to a club in Nottingham, Sarah was part of that same crowd and I feared what I would see her doing and who I would see her doing it with. Sarah had shown me on more than one occasion that she enjoyed making a public spectacle out of humiliating me. I couldn't face it too often, so I started to go out in my local town instead with the lads who I shared the house with.

Every time I did go out in Nottingham, fewer and fewer people would talk to me. That close knit group of friends that I thought I had, distanced themselves. It felt just like the shunning of the congregation all over again. I was being isolated. Only a few people would engage me. The rest would hang their noses up at me. The old camaraderie at the clubs had gone and everyone had split out into their own little factions again. Without me and Ashmi there bringing everyone together, everyone split back into cliques. It was sad to see. I wasn't in any clique, I was alien, on the outside. It was then that I found out that all sorts of rumours were being circulated about me. People who knew me quite closely, who should have known better, thought that all the rumours where true and they distanced themselves from me. Without being actively engaged in the Nottingham and Sheffield scenes, I hadn't been around to defend myself.

That taught me a valuable lesson. I was always prone to take the side of a female when a couple were splitting up. It was always so easy to believe that a man is responsible for doing horrible things and behaving questionably than it is to think that the female is not the innocent party. That stupid rule in clubs and groups - not to get involved - is in fact taking sides and makes us involved. To do nothing and say nothing, makes a statement. I think the majority of the world still doesn't get that.

My waning cultural influence in Nottingham was starting to become evident. I was never any good at the political games and was never interested in them, just interested in people. The Nottingham goth scene became very politicised.

I left 13 Candles as advised by a promoter in Nottingham and struck out on my own with Personality Crisis. I played a couple of gigs in Nottingham and tried to sell my demo cassettes, but the promised support from the promoter disappeared straight away and I soon realised that the advice given to me was a ploy to get me out of 13 Candles so the band could settle down to carry on with their heavy rock trajectory. I had been played and was too stupid and naïve to do anything about it. Without support, and without any money, I was struggling to do anything with my music. I managed to hire a studio in a neighbouring town that subsidised musicians out of work and managed to record an EP. I scraped every penny I could to get it printed onto a white label CD. But without playing gigs to promote it, the whole thing fizzled out.

I honestly thought I had something interesting and different, especially for 1995. It was so frustrating to have that drive, all that passion and all those ideas and not be able to do anything with them. The biggest difficulty was getting other musicians to join me and explore a different sound. Everyone just wanted to do the same as everyone else musically, it was a constant frustration.

## -X-

After about two hours of being slumped, cold, sweating and sickly on the public toilet floor, I started to feel just a little human. A genius idea popped into my head. There was a newspaper kiosk in the underground tunnel across from the public toilets, if I could make it there and buy a chocolate bar, it might give me enough of a sugar rush to help me walk home. I thought about the friends I had left in the café and my poor girlfriend Helen, who would be beside herself with worry about where I was after all that time.

I stood to my feet, opened the cubicle door and slowly made my way to the kiosk to buy a Mars bar, then started the two mile walk home while slowly nibbling at the chocolate bar. I could have taken the bus, but the thought of that and puking up on public transport threatened my anxiety levels again, so I stuck to breathing the fresh air and slowly making my way home. It took another hour to get home to the relief of Helen who was close to ringing the hospitals or the police. My friend had spent two hours running around the city centre trying to find out where I had gone. Bless him.

Helen made sure I went to the doctor. The Doctor sent me to an anxiety management class and gave me a course of counselling, which started to scratch the surface of my unusual upbringing and how I needed to finally face up to my past as a Jehovah's

Witness.

# 17

## SUMMER 2019,
## 48 YEARS OLD

Sam was right, I would find my little goth girl and live happily ever after. We are celebrating 25 years together and 16 years married with a big party and loads of friends. Included in the guest list are a number of former Jehovah's Witnesses, people I used to know, love and be close to that have been strangers for such a long time.

It has taken a long time to come to terms with my past and to try and be at peace with the world around me, but it's still difficult. Some chapters close and other chapters open, even if I don't want them to.

I gave being a free artist the best shot I had, but eventually I had to come to terms with the fact that I couldn't make any sort of living, even a meagre one from my artistry. I knew accepting that fact would mean having to go back into a vocation. I had never worked where I could earn enough money to get off the breadline. I had never had any opportunity to work at anything other than labouring. I heard of many people talk about work giving you a sense of purpose and forging your personality. I also listened to people talk about starting at the bottom and working their way up. Every place I ever worked, the myth that there is reward for hard and honest work echoes around the walls and in the mouths of the employers. But it has always been empty and false. I had hoped that in the eight years I was out of work, returning to work I might see those myths realised. But that was not to be.

Just like the Jehovah's Witnesses, a workplace fits a certain personality type, one that is eager for money and power. If you don't have that personality trait, any independent spirit, any moral backbone is going to be ripped out from you regardless of how hard you work. I went back into work with a strong sense of morality and a strong sense of fairness. It only took a year or two for that sense to be attacked and stripped. I had spent eight years building a self, a personality. Employment took less than a year to destroy it. It's still an internal battle to this day, the fight between standing for moral right and the need to put bread on the table. Every workplace is born out of greed and hunger for power, no matter how much it tries to wear the liberal cloak. Like the majority of middle-class liberalism, it's mostly a lying veneer used to ease the conscience.

While the workplace slowly seems to strip me of personality, the growth to accept my past for what it is makes me stronger.

The spectre of Armageddon followed me for a number of years. The mathematical certainty of the Jehovah's Witnesses being the only religion that had predicted the beginning of the end was a staple of my belief that they were likely right in their faith and I was going to pay for not being one of them. They believe that Jerusalem was destroyed in 607 BC and with that destruction God stopped blessing the Jews as his chosen people. The Jehovah's Witnesses then say that they found a key in the bible that gave 7 periods of 360 years (360 days in a Jewish year, a year for a day) when the start of the end would begin. They gave 1914 as the date when that period would begin and they predicted it before it happened. Part of the signs of that last period would be in wars, earthquakes, pestilence and death to levels never seen in the history of man. They say that all that would be a sign of the end. The Jehovah's Witnesses then give countless examples of how the 20th Century has been the worse period in man's history.

That haunted me for years. I couldn't counter any of it. All of it was truth that had been taught to me for twenty years in the most influential part of my life. All of those were undisputed facts that followed me, like a shadow waiting for the impending Armageddon that was so close you could smell it, where God would destroy all the those not worshipping Jehovah, which included me.

Then Helen and I bought a house and moved in together and I got a Windows computer and an internet connection. It only took a few months before I found a rumour that the Jehovah's Witnesses organisation were paid members of the United Nations. At first, I thought that rumour was ridiculous. Jehovah's Witnesses believe that the United Nations is an abomination on the earth in fulfilment of prophecy. For Jehovah's Witnesses to be paid members of the United Nations, would make them part of that abomination. There was no way it was going to be true.

Then one day I found a website that gave out a direct link to the United Nations website. On that United Nations webpage, it explained that the administration of the United Nations was getting so many requests to see the signed agreement of the Jehovah's Witness organisation with the United Nations organisation that they decided to dedicate a webpage to it so people could get that information for themselves. It included a download of the document which was on public show. So, I downloaded and kept a copy. And there it was in plain sight and undisputed. Jehovah's Witnesses were fully paid members of the United Nations from 1992 to 2001 when the Guardian newspaper exposed their relationship and the organisation pulled out.

That was the most disgusting betrayal of trust for

a member of the Jehovah's Witnesses. Any current Jehovah's Witness will not believe that fact and all would say it was a lie. That opened the floodgates for me. If that was possible, what else could be a lie? I think it was the Geological Society of America's website that I stumbled across next. They had an email contact on their website. And so, considering what I was taught about the change in the earth's activity after 1914, that there was a significant difference in the number and the deaths from volcanoes and earthquakes ever since 1914, I emailed and asked the experts. To my shock, I got a lovely reply from one of their data analysts. She said that there was no change recorded from 1914. The only change came in the twenties when more recording devices were set up around the world so the collection of data became more accurate. In fact, she added that in the earth's history, we are currently going through a bit of a quiet period in terms of crust movement and current geological events. She then added that because science had got better at predicting earthquakes and volcanoes and created technologies to build better homes etc, the number of annual deaths in the twentieth century actually plummeted.

Once again, this was in total opposition to the absolute truth I had been taught through the Jehovah's Witnesses organisation. Once that questioning started, there was no stopping it and I had a sudden realisation of spending decades as a fool. That one mathematical certainty that kept me sure that the Jehovah's Witnesses had the truth, the predicted dates of the fall of Jerusalem in 607 BC and the calculation of 2,520 years to 1914 AD had the simplest flaw that I had overlooked all my life. The count of 2,520 was based on the Jewish year of 360 days, but then the 2,520 years were made in modern year counts. It was so obviously stupid that I couldn't understand why I hadn't seen it before. If you count those 2,520 in 360-day years, it falls short by decades! It's all rubbish, it's all made up.

It was only later I found out that no scholar of history in the world thinks that Jerusalem fell in 607 BC anyway and that's another date made up by Jehovah's Witnesses. To realise it's all lies and deception is heart-breaking but also it has freed me from the guilt and the fear. Armageddon is not coming. I don't need to fear God's wrath. And if that threat is gone, then why do I allow very ordinary men that call themselves Elders to have any power over me? I suppose the eternal question is, why do the Jehovah's Witnesses organisation do what they do, what do they get out of it? I can only suppose that at one time it was to create the biggest book publishing company in the world. The Watchtower always used to be in the Guiness Book of Records for the biggest selling magazine in the world. It isn't anymore. I think like McDonalds, they have now become landowners in place of book publishers, owning massive amounts of land worldwide, which they have been selling off at an alarming rate over the past few years.

Where does all this leave me? Happily married,

still writing music at an incredibly slow rate with Andy as Personality Crisis. I still see myself as a dark romantic and as a goth, but I still haven't found the goths I thought I would meet. I did always think that I would be a love guru in my younger years. A person of intense love, sensuality, warmth, passion, goodness, honesty, a hippy in the truest sense where I could love anyone and everyone intensely. But I think real life has killed so much of that off.

I'm still very much an alien. A person that is so proud to be different and to not be the same as everyone else, but struggles to fight against the world, a world full of liars and cheats. It hurts me personally to see it all the time around me. To find liars and cheats in the organisation I grew up in that taught me not to lie under any circumstance is hard to accept. My mother has lied and cheated so many times and still refuses to come clean with those lies. I have family members that are still Jehovah's Witnesses that have public reputations for being the most awful liars and cheats and its only now I hear about it. I see with my own eyes and ears Governing Body members lie without shame under oath on the Bible to the Australian government during the Australian Royal Commission's investigation into Child Sex Abuse. Each moment is like a knife going into my heart.

I watch sport on the television, and I see footballers cheat by kicking the shins of the opposition and it's called professional fouling. I look at the sport I like, Formula One, and so much of it is about how clever the teams are to find the boundaries of what is legal under the rules, basically how good they are at cheating and getting away with it. My other sports passion is cycling. I've loved cycling since I was 15 years old. When Lance Armstrong came along and won the Tour De France seven times, he was my hero, an athlete I could truly admire, a man that battled against drug abuse and fought and beat testicular cancer. Only to find out he lied and cheated all that time. Lance Armstrong was a liar and a cheat when I saw him win his record sixth tour in 2004 in Paris.

Then every day, I see everyone around me lie and cheat. The streets are full of litter and yet strangely no-one admits to dropping any. No-one admits they break the law and yet no-one can stick to the speed limit in their car. No-one votes Tory but the Tories always have all the votes. Everyone cares about the environment and yet everyone still drives gas guzzlers and produces children uncontrollably.

The heart-breaking part is that I'm becoming part of that society even though it kills part of me to be like that. Having a job is like giving away a piece of your soul each and every day.

But I can take some comfort that I try and preserve my soul as much as I can. I fight the tide and I do see others that fight it too and that is heart-warming. When I took nine pills, there was no-one around that I could turn to that understood. Now in the internet age, there are many groups and organisations in existence that understand what it is like to come out of a cult, to be alien, to be alone.

Don't take the pills, ask for help.

# IF YOU ENJOYED THIS BOOK, PLEASE GIVE THE FOLLOWING SOME CONSIDERATION

**Sophie Lancaster foundation**

Sophie Lancaster was a young woman who was murdered for being different. She and her boyfriend were creative, artistic people who dressed in their own unique way. They were attacked by a gang of five boys in a park in Bacup, Lancashire on 11 August 2007. The gang attacked Sophie's boyfriend first and then turned on her, carrying out a brutal and sustained attack. Sophie remained in hospital for 13 days, before following medical advice, the family agreed to life support being switched off. Sophie died on 24 August 2007; she was just 20 years old.

Sophie's mother, Sylvia, had seen at first-hand the abuse and prejudice her daughter had previously been subjected to, because of how she dressed. During the long hours at hospital, Sylvia decided that when Sophie was better, they would go into schools and talk to young people about difference, and how it is ok to be who you are and express yourself in your own way. Sadly, Sylvia never got a chance to do this with Sophie.

Sylvia was determined that she would carry on this work and The Sophie Lancaster Foundation was established as a lasting legacy to a beautiful life cut short by violence. The charity works to promote tolerance and acceptance for others – however we are different, and champions alternative people in our communities. The Foundation's mission to stamp out prejudice hatred and intolerance everywhere, can be summed up in one word.

S.O.P.H.I.E

https://www.sophielancasterfoundation.com/

# USEFUL INFORMATION

If you need more information about Jehovah's Witnesses

jwfacts.com

If you need support after leaving Jehovah's witnesses or any other high control religious group

www.faithtofaithless.com
www.recoveringfromreligion.org

Other interesting sources of information

www.youtube.com/Jexit_2020
jwwatch.org

If you have left the Jehovah's Witnesses or are thinking of leaving, there are lots of caring and understanding social media groups to be found on the internet. It is no small thing leaving such a highly controlling organisation and there are always consequences. To seek help is not only advisable, it is essential, as you will not be fully aware of the impact that your indoctrination has had on you.

I strongly recommend seeking professional guidance through counselling. Be aware also that there are many counsellors themselves that are not aware of the damaging effects of highly controlling religious groups and on those trying to escape them. Please direct any counsellors that wish to seek advice to contact www.faithtofaithless.com

## ABOUT THE AUTHOR

Jonny Halfhead was born into the Jehovah's Witnesses organisation. He was a third generation Jehovah's Witness publisher until the age of 20.
He started starting writing books after the realisation that those first 20 years as a Jehovah's Witness were anything but ordinary. He now writes to expose the dangerous controlling practices of the Jehovah's Witnesses organisation and is proud to call himself an Activist

www.jonnyhalfhead.com

Other works by this author:

# Nine Pills

# The 1975 Apocalypse

# The Offence of Grace

Printed in Great Britain
by Amazon